"G⋯⋯ her⋯⋯ between them. Because yeah, her body wanted me—as evidenced by the slickness now coating my groin. Slickness that had nothing to do with the shallow water beneath her legs.

I ignored her command and issued one of my own. "Start. Talking."

It was an order that shouldn't be very hard for Riley to follow, as the woman usually had no problem speaking her mind.

Yet now, of all times, she chose to remain silent.

And mutinously glare up at me.

While simultaneously pressing up into my cock with an obvious invitation to fuck.

It was an invitation I would accept *after* we discussed her antics.

"Riley," I growled, ensuring she understood that I wasn't in the mood to be denied. Not with her sweet and *wet* body beneath me. "I'm about five seconds away from knotting you, *Omega*. Explain to me how that's even possible."

I already knew the cause—*suppressants*.

What I really wanted was for her to explain *why*.

She swallowed, some of the fire dying in her gaze.

I narrowed my eyes. "Answer me. Tell me why you took suppressants." Maybe informing her of what I obviously knew already would help her open up.

"I… I wanted a life…" The soft words weren't the ones I'd expected to hear, causing me to frown. I'd never heard her speak in that tone before. It made her that much more *Omega*.

And I wasn't sure if I liked it.

Riley was all feisty prowess, which I admired about her.

I didn't want her meek and submissive. I simply wanted *her*.

"I wanted to *live*," she continued with a little more power, some part of her seeming to snap into place again. "To be more than a pup-maker."

My eyebrows flew upward. "More than a *what?*"

"You heard me," she replied, her blue eyes gleaming with liquid fire once more.

There's my girl, I thought. *Keep talking.*

X-CLAN
SERIES

X-CLAN

The Origin

USA TODAY BESTSELLING AUTHOR
LEXI C. FOSS

X-Clan: The Origin

Editing by: Outthink Editing, LLC

Proofreading by: Katie Schmahl & Jean Bachen

Cover Design: Jay R. Villalobos with Covers by Juan

Cover Photography: CJC Photography

Cover Models: Gus Caleb Smyrnios & Riley Rebecca

Published by: Ninja Newt Publishing, LLC

Print Edition

ISBN: 978-1-68530-144-6

❈ Created with Vellum

X-CLAN
THE ORIGIN

X-CLAN
THE ORIGIN

**The compound walls have been breached.
The Infected are upon us.
There is no cure. Nowhere to hide. The only
option is to *run*.**

Alpha Jonas is my sexy-as-sin guard.
The one assigned to protect me from a world doomed by
chaos and disease.
Now he promises to escort me to safety.

There's just one problem.
He doesn't know that I'm an Omega.

And not just any Omega.
An Omega who is about to go into heat.

I've spent my entire life hiding from my fate.
But in our haste to flee, I left my suppressants behind.

I can either accept the inevitable.
Or take my chances with the Infected.

Because once Alpha Jonas learns what I am…
He won't just knot me.
He'll claim me.

A NOTE FROM LEXI

The X-Clan series takes place in a shared universe where supernaturals live in various sectors throughout the world. Their paranormal identities were revealed shortly after a zombielike virus began infecting the human population.

Some of the supernaturals are impacted by the virus. Others—like the X-Clan wolves—are not.

And, unfortunately, humans are not immune.

When the X-Clan series begins, over 90% of the human population has been altered by this virus.

Thus, it's a dark future.

However, I've always wanted to go back to the origin to explore life during that time.

Those of you who have read the X-Clan series will be familiar with Riley and Jonas, as they are key characters in that world. This is the story of how they ended up together. And it's written in a way that those unfamiliar with the X-Clan world can easily jump in to follow along.

X-Clan: The Origin is a standalone prequel that provides history for the shifter universe and explores the love connection between one of the most influential couples in the X-Clan world.

I hope you enjoy Jonas and Riley's story!

Hugs,
Lexi

P.S. On a personal note, this story was inspired by my graduate degree in Public Health. Epidemiology has always fascinated me, and I conceptualized this entire world in 2019, prior to writing *Andorra Sector*. So this story was in no way inspired by current events. <3

PROLOGUE

JONAS

Doctor Riley Campbell is a brat.

She's unruly. Uncooperative. Rude. And the most alluring wolf I've ever had the displeasure of meeting.

I don't know what her fucking problem is, but one of these days, I'm going to bend that rebellious little Beta over my knee and spank her ass raw.

Then fuck her.

For days.

And days.

Until this obsession with the sweet-smelling doctor leaves my system.

I've never been this attracted to a female, let alone a Beta. But there is just something about Riley that calls to my wolf.

I've tried to ignore it.

But she's constantly provoking my inner dominant with her sassy little remarks and snarky comments.

I can smell her interest in me, which is perhaps the

heart of our problem. So a good fuck will solve this issue for both of us.

Or worsen it.

That's assuming she allows me to protect her long enough for both of us to survive this hell.

At the rate we're going, we're both going to end up dead in months.

Because she refuses to listen to my directives and she fights me every step of the way.

I'm not a bad Alpha, little wolf.
If you give me a chance, you'll see how good I can be to you.
So why don't you put the claws away? Let me pet you. Show you what
I can do with my hands and my tongue.
I promise you'll feel worshipped in the end.
Because I'll treat you like a queen.
And leave you begging me for more…

CHAPTER 1
RILEY

CDC COMPOUND

"What the hell is wrong with you?" I demanded, glaring at my reflection in the mirror. "You shouldn't need another suppressant already."

My wolf stared back at me, the darkening orbs confirming what I already knew—my heat was coming. *Again.*

I'd just taken a suppressant three months ago. I shouldn't need another one already.

It's Jonas, I thought. *That damn insufferable Alpha is driving my inner Omega crazy.*

My wolf had been acting up since the day he'd arrived thirteen months ago.

He was here to guard me. Which only made the situation worse. Because my animal practically melted beneath his protective vibes.

Fuck.

5

I gripped the countertop, the svelte muscles along my arms flexing.

I used to take one or two suppressants a year. They masked my scent and quelled my mating instincts. But I'd already taken *four* since Jonas's arrival.

And it was definitely his presence that set me off. I'd been around several other Alphas over the last decade, and I'd never had this problem before.

Of course, none of those Alphas had been X-Clan wolves, so perhaps that was the real issue—having an Alpha of my own kind around.

He thought I was a Beta. Everyone did.

Well, everyone except for Kieran. His affinity for healing had clued him in to my natural traits almost immediately. However, he'd agreed to remain quiet for my benefit.

Or perhaps for his benefit, too.

Because the second my true nature was revealed, I'd be claimed by an X-Clan Alpha and forced into a nest. That was what my kind did—they cherished Omegas yet coerced them into breeding roles.

No professional opportunities.

No life outside of the nest.

No *choices*.

Just a pampered existence with a doting Alpha.

Or, in my case, a trio of Alphas, if my father's earlier arrangements in my life had come to fruition.

Perhaps not a terrible way to live, but I had too many aspirations to just allow myself to be claimed.

That was why I'd run.

Why I'd left my pack and pursued my own path.

It had been going well.

At least until the Infection had begun.

I hung my head on a sigh. *Even more reason to take another suppressant.* I couldn't focus on my research while in heat.

Not that we were close to discovering a cure, though. No, we were far from that prospect, what with the amoebae eating through every fucking solution we devised.

It was just mutating too quickly.

Destroying everything in its path.

And essentially reacting just like it did in its host by *eating* wildly without any thought.

Zombiism, the humans called it.

Infection was my chosen term.

Over sixty percent of the world had been destroyed already. My unit was the only one left searching for a cure. And it wasn't a coincidence that most of us weren't human.

We had a few mortals in our lab, but not many. They were just too susceptible to—

I winced as a horn blared overhead, the sound vibrating the air and stirring the hairs along my arms.

"What the…?" But I didn't need to finish my question, as I already knew the reason for the alarm. "*Shit.*"

That sound indicated a breach in the compound walls.

Which meant evacuation was imminent.

There were just too many Infected. Once they caught a scent, they stopped at nothing to achieve a taste. And it seemed that it didn't matter how many walls or layers existed between us and them; they could still scent us. Almost as though they were wolves themselves.

Of course this has to happen today of all days.

I darted back into my bedroom to grab my escape bag and carried it into the bath area, where I kept my suppressants. I should have just taken one when I'd woken up with a headache. Instead, I'd wasted time being mad at my wolf and debating the need for another dose already.

7

Stupid, Riley.

There wasn't time now for a safe injection, so I packed away the supplies and returned to my room to look for something to wear.

I dropped my towel and grabbed a shirt just as the door to my quarters burst open.

Jonas stood on the threshold, his light blue eyes landing on my naked form in an instant.

Nudity didn't usually bother me as a shifter. But an inane part of me jumped into action as I tried to cover myself with the shirt in my hands.

Jonas either didn't notice or didn't care. "We need to go."

"What do you think I'm doing?" I snapped. "Taking a nap?"

He arched a light brow in response, his silence saying everything and nothing at the same time. He never reacted to my snarky remarks or incessant need to push him away.

Always patient.

Always brooding.

Always *staring.*

I forced my hands to move as I grabbed a pair of black pants to go with my blouse and then opened a drawer for undergarments.

Jonas watched my every move, his nostrils flaring.

"Stare much?" The taunt slid from my mouth on instinct, my penchant for provoking him shining through. I harbored this intrinsic need to irritate him as much as he irritated me, which wasn't fair to him at all and probably made me a brat. But he provoked my wolf. So I provoked him.

He responded to my antics as he usually did—with a grunt—and pushed off the door frame to move into my room.

I took an involuntary step back, my wolf immediately submitting to the Alpha prowling toward me.

Except he moved right past me to pick up my bag and headed for the door without a word.

My nose twitched, telling me he hadn't gone far, just to the hallway to wait. This must have been his version of privacy.

Good.

I needed space.

Because the alarm did nothing to cool my desire for him. *Why does he have to be so big and Alpha-y?*

Oh, right.

Because he's my Alpha bodyguard.

A scrawny wolf wouldn't qualify for the job. While I could take care of myself in most situations, I didn't stand a chance against an army of Infected. And the International Council had deemed my background as one that required protection.

Hence, they'd assigned Jonas to me.

My doctoral background in infectious disease and epidemiology marked me as valuable. And the fact that I was one of the few still alive made me even more important to the cause.

Most of my former colleagues had been human, which hadn't boded well for them when dealing with the brain-eating amoeba that continued to mutate each time it reached a new host.

One bite and the virus spread.

There were even some wolves that it could infect, like the Ash Wolves.

Not X-Clan or V-Clan wolves, though.

But that didn't stop the Infected from trying to make a lunch out of us when they had a chance. We didn't die easily. However, we could be severely injured and eventually die if we were surrounded by too many Infected.

Which was why I had Jonas.

Big, powerful, muscular Jonas.

With his long blond hair, chiseled jaw, icy irises, and pale skin.

He even had a slight accent. *Icelandic*. Because he'd grown up near Blood Sector in Iceland. I only knew that because Kieran had mentioned it.

Jonas didn't talk much.

He liked to grunt and growl and *stare*.

I considered his piercing gaze while I dressed, wondering what he'd thought about while watching me moments ago. He hadn't smelled interested, but he hadn't appeared bored either. There'd been a slight flare in his nostrils and a subtle dilation of his pupils.

Can he sense my approaching heat? I wondered as I pulled on a tank top over my bra. Then I busied myself with buttoning up my blouse before putting on a thong and my black pants. Socks and flat shoes went on next—in case I needed to run.

I tossed my damp hair up into a ponytail and debated adding perfume to kill my scent.

But that could also attract the Infected.

So no.

I'd just have to deal with this flight and either find a place to inject my suppressant on the plane or locate a secure place once we landed.

Maybe I can get on Kieran's plane, I thought, grabbing my purse—which only had my international military ID and a satellite phone in it—and heading toward the door.

Jonas stood outside, his gaze vigilant and his posture prepared for battle.

I held out my hand. "I can take my bag."

He grunted again and shifted on his heel, ignoring me.

"I'm not weak," I told him as I followed. "And there's barely anything in that escape kit. I can carry it."

He didn't reply, instead leading me down the white corridor of the residence hall.

We were deep underground here, which meant we needed to head up to reach the airfield.

The alarms outside confirmed it was those walls that had been breached. It would take hours, if not days, for the Infected to find a way to tunnel their way to us. There was a chance they'd never make it.

But the airfield was a very different story.

We had a significant army upstairs that was likely in the process of protecting the grounds.

And shooting everything that moves, I thought, my mood plummeting.

The brain-eating amoeba had mutated into a disease that made humans mindless flesh-eaters. And I'd spent the better part of the last five years trying to find a solution.

While humans just… killed each other.

That was their solution—to battle what they didn't understand and remove the wounded rather than help them.

Jonas glanced down at me as he called for the elevator, his gaze assessing.

I didn't remark on his penchant for staring this time.

I just focused on the slatted doors as they opened, and stepped inside, resigned to the fate that awaited us above ground.

Jonas stood in front of me, blocking my view and taking on a protective position as we began to ascend. He dropped my bag to the floor and pulled out a gun, his stance telling me he was focused on whatever he heard above.

I didn't allow myself to listen.

I'd been living with screams for too long.

Sobs. Unfathomable sounds. *Death*.

I shivered, the urge to wrap my arms around myself hitting me hard. But I knew better than to give in to the sensation of desolation.

Crying didn't solve the situation.

Nothing did, I thought sourly. *Nothing works. Nothing fixes this. The humans let it mutate beyond repair.*

I hated blaming them, but I couldn't help it. The mortal politicians were the ones who had turned the outbreak into a political debate rather than a public health discussion.

They hadn't listened to the researchers or the physicians in charge. They'd only attempted to speak from their sides of the political playing field.

And the whole world had paid for their ignorance.

A wave of balmy air hit me as the doors opened, the Georgia heat overwhelming and unwelcome. We were about ninety miles northeast of Atlanta, having taken refuge in an underground facility very few knew about near the border with North Carolina.

But from the sounds echoing outside, it was clear that a horde of Infected had come in from the city and found us here in the hills of the Appalachian Mountains.

Gunshots reverberated through the air, making me wince.

Shouts followed.

I closed my eyes and stole a deep breath. *There's nothing you can do to save them right now. Just survive and keep searching.* It was a mantra I often repeated to—

A heavy hand landed on my lower back, yanking me back into the present.

"Follow me," Jonas said, his lips suddenly against my ear as he escorted me out of the elevator.

He'd retrieved my bag, tucked away his gun, and had me against his side in an instant.

Or maybe I'd frozen when the doors had opened.

I really wasn't sure, but my legs were moving now as he guided me toward the waiting jets.

Screeches and gunfire followed, the collective noise making me weak. I hated what this world had become. Hated that I couldn't fix it. Hated that my genetics allowed me to survive while so many innocents *died*.

It wasn't until I peered up a set of metal stairs that I remembered I had wanted to find Kieran's plane. But it was too late.

Jonas was already pushing me onto this jet.

And I would be a fool to demand he take me elsewhere.

A human pilot was already on board, his fear creating an acrid stench that upset my wolf. I nearly growled, but Jonas's presence at my back instantly calmed my urge.

This is why he's dangerous, I thought deliriously. *He grounds me too easily.*

Which made sense. He was an Alpha. That was what they did.

But they were also capable of a lot of destruction.

They took what they wanted however they wanted it.

Like Omegas.

I curled into myself as Jonas escorted me to a seat, my urge to melt and hide overwhelming my ability to process my surroundings. His nearness only heightened the very real signs of my impending heat. It was almost as though him being beside me sped up the process inside me.

An impossibility, one I knew was a ridiculous notion as a practicing physician.

But that didn't stop my brain from wondering if his knot had some sort of magic voodoo that deepened my impending lust.

Fucking hormones, I thought as he buckled me in, his woodsy scent overwhelming me with the movements. *I can handle my own seat belt*, I wanted to say. But the words were stuck to the roof of my mouth as another horrendous scream met my ears.

How many of them are dying out there? Gunned down by their fellow humans?

I knew they didn't have a choice at this point. The Infected outnumbered the Uninfected now. And it was only getting worse.

It was a survive-or-die mentality.

I just hated that the world had allowed itself to degrade to this level of destruction.

Many supernaturals were developing protective regions in response to the epidemic. They weren't safe areas for humans, though. Only for their own kind.

Everyone had a "look out for myself" approach to the world these days.

Given everything I'd witnessed, I couldn't blame them. The humans hadn't exactly earned our help in this matter.

But that didn't stop me from trying to make a difference.

At least, it hadn't, anyway.

However, it was starting to seem pointless.

The door to the jet closed, leaving just me and Jonas in the back with the single pilot up front.

"We're not taking anyone else?" I asked, looking out the window at the military personnel battling in our wake.

"They'll be on the cargo planes," Jonas explained, his deep voice unnaturally soft. "They prioritized research personnel first."

"Where's Kieran?"

Jonas grunted, his icy blue eyes leaving my face as he looked out the window beside him. "On another plane."

I sighed. If Kieran were on the jet, he could have distracted Jonas for me. I wasn't sure I could inject myself with Jonas nearby, let alone reach my suppressants. I should have put them in my purse, not my main bag.

Although, I didn't even have my purse with me now.

"Where did you put my stuff?" I asked, realizing that Jonas had taken my purse at some point and put everything away before buckling me in. There were only two rows of chairs, making this a four-seater. Therefore, my bag couldn't be far.

I wonder if there's a bathroom in the back. Or a bedroom? Because this was clearly a repurposed luxury jet, probably taken from a former human celebrity or billionaire. *Maybe I can grab my pack and head back there?*

"Bulkhead," Jonas muttered, gesturing with his chin toward a shelving unit just behind us.

"And where are we heading?" I asked as the jet began to move toward the tarmac. This whole area had once been one of the government's hidden bases in the United States, the underground bunker designed specifically for the purpose of highly classified research.

There weren't many locations like this left for us to go to. Hence my question. I also wanted to know if there was time for me to grab my bag and disappear into the bathroom.

"East." Jonas didn't elaborate, his attention having shifted to the pilot.

My nose twitched, aware of what he was smelling. *Fear. Pain. Terror.*

It was a common stench in my lab, but that didn't make me any more used to it.

Jonas remained quiet as the plane ascended, his eyes narrowing a little when the scent didn't change.

I frowned. "What is it?" I kept my voice low, aware that the pilot couldn't hear us back here over the roar of the engines.

Jonas didn't reply but unbuckled his seat belt and leaned forward a little, his nostrils flaring.

I glanced between him and the pilot.

Then I caught a new scent, one that reminded me of dead flesh.

My mouth went dry. *Oh, no...*

I knew that scent far too well.

There's an Infected on the plane.

Jonas stood, his shoulders rolling as he loosened his stance.

Then he pulled the gun from his hip.

And aimed.

Right at the pilot's head.

"Jonas," I hissed. "If you miss—"

The pilot began to convulse, causing Jonas to curse.

"You'll depressurize the plane!" I shouted as he started forward, gun still raised.

But he wasn't listening to me. He was focused on the now snarling human.

I couldn't even see where he'd been bitten. However, now that I was paying attention, I could smell the infection.

Damn.

No wonder he'd been exuding terror. He'd been bitten and knew what was about to happen.

These fucking mortals. They continued to make bad decisions, which was what had spread the virus in the first place!

The Cheyenne Mountain Complex, a site that was formerly regarded as one of the safest locations in the

17

world, had been taken down by a senator. He'd been bitten, hadn't told anyone, and proceeded to change once *inside* the mountain complex.

By then, it'd been too late to do anything about it.

Because he'd bitten a handful of humans.

Who'd bitten more humans.

And it had spiraled from there.

But to make matters worse, half of the Infected were former military. Which meant they weren't just mindless creatures trying to eat their way out of the mountain. They were *armed* creatures who instinctively knew how to fire a gun.

While also wanting to eat everything in their path.

Not all the human faculties died with the virus, but the part that deciphered between right and wrong did.

And the virus itself turned the hosts into cannibals—hence the *zombie* term—while removing their senses of danger and morality.

It also impacted other neurological areas, such as speech patterns, which was evidenced now by the pilot trying to defend himself against Jonas.

There were a series of garbled words coming from his mouth that sounded oddly like an apology.

"Just a scratch," he seemed to be saying.

That's all it takes, I thought sadly. This was part of the mutation—it spread so easily now that some researchers feared it might become airborne, if it wasn't already.

There were also those of my kind who feared it might evolve enough to start impacting all supernatural beings. That worry only increased after the Ash Wolves had begun to react to the virus.

Luckily, it hadn't shown signs of spreading to many others yet.

But with how fast everything seemed to change, who

knew where we'd be in a century, let alone a decade from now, or even next year.

The pilot slurred something unintelligible and swung upright, his arm knocking several controls along the way and pitching the jet harshly to the side.

I yelped, my nails digging into the leathery arms as Jonas crashed into the side of the plane. *Shit!*

He released a roar that made my knees shake, my inner wolf immediately bowing to his command. *Oh, moons...*

His woodsy scent overwhelmed the air around me, the Alpha allowing his dominant side out to play in a way I hadn't seen before. I had no idea just how subdued he usually was... until now.

Until he shoved off the side of the plane and charged toward the pilot.

His steps were sure, his movements fluid and honed by decades of experience. Maybe even longer. I had no clue how old Jonas was, just that he was older than me.

And far more powerful.

His leather jacket strained against his muscles as he took the pilot down, his big hands wrapping around the human's head and twisting it violently.

The snap reached my ears, even over the engine's vibrations, the sound of the neck breaking sending a chill down my spine.

So easy.

So immediate.

And yet the jet was angled in a way that was going to kill us if we didn't do something quickly.

I started to unbuckle my seat belt, but Jonas stilled me with a lethal look. "*Stay.*" The word wrapped around me like a noose, demanding my submission.

I held up my hands to show that I was obeying.

And he made his way to the cockpit.

"Do you even know how to fly a plane?" The words came out in a low mutter, the question one I wasn't sure I actually wanted an answer to.

But he'd clearly heard it because he threw an icy glower back at me over his shoulder before he settled into the pilot's seat and began fiddling with the controls.

I clutched my stomach as he did something to stabilize the trajectory of the plane. *Ugh.* The room spun a little. Or the plane did. Or just my mind. I really wasn't sure.

Vertigo, the physician part of me recognized. *Really bad vertigo.*

I tried to focus enough to see, but my vision was painted in black stripes.

Really hope Jonas can see, I thought dizzily. *Really hope he knows… what… he's doing…*

My insides rioted as we continued through the sky, and I only vaguely heard a voice saying, "You're going to have to walk me through that."

"No shit."

"Where am I heading?"

"Go—" A fuzzy sound followed, the echoing making me wince.

"Didn't catch that, Kieran." Jonas's voice was clearer, but I couldn't see him, my vision still unfocused. "Kieran? *Fuck.*"

The atmosphere changed again, making me queasy.

"We need to land." The words were clear, Jonas's voice loud. But I didn't know if they were for me or Kieran.

Is he talking to him on the comms? Is that what they're even called on a plane? I wasn't sure.

"Whatever you do, don't get up," Jonas added.

That must have been for me. Rather than acknowledge him, I just tried to sink into my seat a little more to keep from throwing up.

Not that I had any food in my stomach to lose.

I'd missed breakfast, thanks to my internal suppressant debate.

Something I was a bit thankful for now as the plane dipped again. I didn't typically suffer from motion sickness, but nothing about this felt normal.

Jonas cursed.

Kieran's voice came through again, the communication scratchy.

I couldn't decipher what he said, but Jonas responded with what sounded like coordinates.

Then he shouted for me to hold on.

To what? I wanted to ask, my arms curling around myself as my seat belt held me captive. *This is really not how I want to die.*

Wolf or not, I doubted we could survive a plane crash.

We healed quickly, but not that quickly.

The plane shook violently, the change in air pressure irritating my ears. *Fuck. Fuck. Fuck.*

A growl vibrated through the cabin, the source coming from Jonas. I shivered in response, my wolf whimpering inside.

This is bad.

Very, very bad.

Why didn't we check the pilot?

How was he bitten?

Fuck!

I jerked in the chair as the wings shifted and the wheels squealed beneath the plane.

My eyes flew open, but vertigo still painted my vision in dark spots. However, I could sense enough to know that he'd just engaged the landing gear.

We're going too fast.

Too fast.

We're going to crash!

Another growl sounded, followed by a sharp rumble that stole the air from my lungs. *A purr.*

No. No, that couldn't be right.

Why would Jonas purr?

Except that was exactly what I heard. A soft, soothing *purr.*

I released my abdomen to grab the arms of the chair again. His purr continued to rumble through the jet, the speakers seeming to amplify it.

Why is he doing that?

Is he… is he trying to soothe me?

Am I losing my mind?

I brought my hand up to my head, but a jerking movement had me gripping the chair once more. "Jonas…"

"Just breathe, Riley," he replied, the loudness of his voice confirming he'd turned on the speaker somehow.

His purr continued, the sound wrapping around me in a warm blanket of familiarity. I hadn't heard an Alpha purr in years. Maybe a decade or more. And that purr hadn't been meant for me, but for another shifter.

Yet this one…

This Alpha is purring for me.

My inner wolf instantly calmed, my world feeling unmistakably right.

Only, a harsh jolt of the plane jerked me out of my peaceful state, making my teeth chatter as the screeching sound of brakes filled the air.

We're on the ground, I realized. *He… he landed the plane. He actually landed the plane!*

His purr morphed into another growl as he fought with the controls to come to a stop, the severe grating sound unlike anything I'd ever heard.

And then we paused, everything falling still.

An exhale whooshed from my lungs, my mind fighting to catch up to everything that had just happened.

Jonas was still strapped into the pilot's chair—I had no idea when he'd buckled himself in, but he was secure and facing forward.

The pilot was dead.

And we—I peered out the windows—seemed to be at an old airport. Or at least on a very long runway with posts that reminded me of those lights that used to flicker at night to designate the landing strip. Only it was early morning with the sun still rising, illuminating everything in its path.

Including a long building that resembled an airport with its gates and ramps.

Behind it appeared to be trees, but I could smell the Infected. Their rotting flesh left a stench in the air that my wolf immediately noticed, causing my mouth to go dry.

Where are we?

It wasn't Atlanta. And we'd only been in the air for maybe twenty minutes at the most.

Were we in Asheville?

Charlotte?

Somewhere in South Carolina?

Jonas moved from the front of the cabin, his icy gaze immediately finding mine as he evaluated me. He'd lost his leather jacket at some point, leaving him in a white shirt and jeans. Given it was probably a hundred degrees outside, that seemed more appropriate.

But he wasn't sweating.

He was just bulging with adrenaline, his Alpha wolf pulsing close to his skin. He didn't speak, just studied my throat, my chest, my waist, and then my face, and nodded. "We need to move," he said, pulling off his shirt.

My eyebrows lifted. "What are you doing?"

"Shifting," he replied, all traces of his purr gone.

I must have been imagining it.

Jonas's hand went to his belt, his muscles rippling. "You need to shift, Riley."

I blinked at him. "What?"

"We need to *run*," he explained. "In wolf form. Straight into the woods. We'll make it to the base on foot."

My lips parted. "*What?*"

I wasn't an idiot. I'd heard him just fine.

But shifting? Now? While on the verge of going into heat? Not only did that mean leaving my suppressants here —I couldn't carry my bag while in wolf form—but it also meant metabolizing what little serum I had left in my body. "No. I can't shift."

He paused, the top button of his pants undone. "Excuse me?"

"There has to be another way. We have our bags. I can't… We can't… There has to be another way."

Jonas stared at me for a beat. "Get up."

"Jonas."

"*Now.*" The dominance underlining that single word had my hands moving before my mind could process the action.

"Don't you go all growly Alpha on me," I snapped, even while I unbuckled myself and stood. "I'm *not* your subordinate."

He grunted and caught my hip when I started to sway. I hadn't been prepared for the weakness in my limbs, nor had I really been processing my motions while moving.

Because my inner wolf was doing what the Alpha had demanded without thought.

Traitor, I thought at my Omega side.

She responded by leaning toward Jonas, my nostrils flaring at his woodsy scent.

Stop that, I told her. *He is not ours.*

Fortunately, Jonas didn't seem to notice. He was too busy urging me to move out of the aisle and toward the front of the plane. My legs resembled jelly beneath me, the unexpected landing wreaking havoc on my limbs.

Although, that could also be from the upcoming heat.

Or perhaps a combination of all of the above.

Today is not turning into a good day, I muttered to myself. It was a thought that evolved into an even deeper truth as Jonas pointed toward the windows at the front of the plane.

"Now will you shift, princess?" he asked, his tone silky and underlined with a hint of mockery.

My lips parted, words escaping me.

Because *fuck*.

There was an army of Infected ambling toward us. At least a hundred of them. Maybe more. "We... we need..."

"To run," Jonas finished for me. "And we're fastest in wolf form."

I was going to suggest we fly or grab a car or something even faster than being on all fours.

But we'd landed here for a reason.

And we obviously couldn't camp out in this jet.

Unless... "Does Kieran know where we are?"

Jonas released me. "Even if he did, he's not coming for us. We're on our own until we reach the base."

"Why can't he double back and pick us up?" I asked, very aware of my indignant undertone. I really didn't mean to come off as such a brat with Jonas. It was just a natural response to his nearness. His hotness. His... his *Alpha-y* presence.

"Because it's too dangerous." Jonas caught my chin

and forced my gaze to his. "Stop being difficult, Doctor. It's my job to protect you. Which does, in fact, make you my subordinate for the foreseeable future. Now get over yourself and *shift*. Or I'll make you shift. You feel me?"

I gaped at him, torn between fury and shock. In the end, shock won because that was the longest he'd ever spoken to me.

Jonas was a man of few words.

Yet he'd just delivered a speech.

One that ended in a threat regarding his intention to force my shift, which should have infuriated me more than it did, but he wasn't wrong in his statements.

I was being unfair to him and difficult for no reason.

Well, not a reason he understood, anyway. A reason I couldn't exactly explain without revealing my Omega identity.

Which would lead to an entirely different conversation.

I nibbled my lip. The suppressant didn't just quell my Omega instincts and heat; it calmed my wolf. Which meant I might not be able to shift if I injected myself now.

And I couldn't exactly take the serum with me in my mouth. That would be dangerous for a lot of reasons. I would likely need my teeth to break through that horde of Infected outside.

Shit.

Jonas was right. I needed to shift—something I wouldn't have been able to easily do right now had I taken my inoculation this morning. So perhaps my doubt was a result of fate.

But this put me in a complicated situation.

One that would likely reveal my identity to Jonas.

"Riley." The growl in his voice told me he wouldn't be asking again. If I didn't start obeying, he'd take over.

And I would only have myself to blame for whatever

came next.

I'm so fucked, I thought as I started unbuttoning my blouse.

Jonas had already shucked off his pants and shoes, his groin barely covered by a scrap of black boxer shorts.

I tried not to stare.

And failed.

Because he really was an impressive specimen.

Yeah, really, really, really fucked, I clarified to myself.

Because my inner wolf was practically panting already, and I wasn't even in heat yet.

I didn't have much of an option. I could confide the truth and admit my Omega status, but it would do nothing to save us from this current situation. If anything, it would make things worse.

Right, then. Shift. Run. Find shelter. Hide.

And pray my heat didn't kick in before we reached our final destination.

Wherever that might be.

Cursing under my breath, I finished stripping while Jonas observed with an unreadable stare. It was on the tip of my tongue to snap at him again, but I swallowed the urge.

He was right—I needed to let him do his job.

Sighing, I called upon my inner animal and gave her the freedom to take over. She eagerly agreed, my limbs bending on instinct as the shift overwhelmed my being.

Jonas didn't move, his icy gaze on me the whole time.

And still entirely unreadable.

My animal ignored him, instead stretching and shivering at the sensation of being in control after several months of suppressing my need to shift.

Jonas squatted, his gaze meeting mine. "Are you going to be able to run?"

I snorted at him. *Of course I can run.*

"It's obvious you haven't shifted in a while," he added, his hand lifting as though to touch me. But he dropped his palm before he reached my head.

If I could frown, I would. *Obvious how? Is there something wrong with my fur?* I glanced down at my legs and found smooth reddish-brown fur. I danced around to test my balance and felt sturdy on my paws.

I supposed I was a little thin.

But that came with the territory of being an Omega.

Jonas studied me for another minute and stood. "If you need me to slow down, howl."

I snorted again. *I can keep up, Alpha. Trust me.*

Yeah, it'd been a bit since my last shift. And I might be small. But I was fast.

He shrugged and kicked off his boxers, giving me a nice view of, well, *everything.* My wolf practically purred in response, not that I could make that sound. Only Alphas could. However, she openly admired him.

The aggressive energy wafting off the man didn't help matters, either.

He was all dominant male.

"Follow me," he said, heading toward the door to unlatch it. Then he hopped out of the plane to the ground below—*without* a ramp or stairs.

I gaped at him, noting the drop, and wondered exactly how he expected me to *follow* him.

"It's only about eleven or twelve feet," he said. "Jump, Riley."

My wolf wanted to decline that command.

But the screeching sounds coming from the Infected had me obeying on impulse.

"Good girl," Jonas said when my paws hit the concrete. "Now let's see how fast you can run."

CHAPTER 3
JONAS

Riley vibrated with anxiety beside me, her nose twitching as she picked up the scent of decayed flesh in the air.

Or I assumed that was the cause, anyway.

Because I could barely smell anything other than the acrid stench of zombie meat.

What a fucking mess.

The compound had been breached, something that had happened because a human had let a group inside without properly vetting them.

All it took was one infected mortal to spread the virus.

And it had.

As evidenced by the now dead pilot.

I'd picked up a hint of something wrong in his scent. But it'd been a few seconds too late, and we'd already been in the air by the time I'd realized the cause.

Fuck.

I ran a hand down my face and focused on our

surroundings once more. Being off the jet allowed me to see more than I'd been able to from the cockpit.

A good thing because my nose was useless at the moment.

We'd landed just outside of Asheville. Thus, we were close to the mountains yet also near a former tourist hotspot.

Which meant there would be a lot of Infected humans.

But a myriad of trees to provide cover as well.

We just needed to cross through the barrier of zombielike mortals and head east toward Fort Bragg.

The base had a minimal operating crew, mostly there to protect military families and the few fortunate civilians who had managed to reach the protective barrier.

I'd told Kieran we would make our way there to wait for a new aircraft.

He'd agreed with the plan, as Asheville wasn't easily accessible right now. And, as our jet had been one of the last to leave the CDC compound, it wouldn't be easy for anyone to come to retrieve us now.

Therefore, we were on our own for the time being.

And we had a good two-hundred-fifty-mile adventure ahead of us.

If we could find a car, that would be best.

Otherwise, we'd be making the trip on four paws.

If we went at a decent pace, we could make it there in five or six days. We'd have to find safe places to rest, though. And that would be the tricky part of this journey.

Well, and surviving the Infected coming toward us.

Hmm.

It would have been easier to use the weapons on the plane and just gun down a bunch of Infected, then run through the hole created by their deaths.

But Riley harbored a soft spot for the Infected. I

supposed that instinct came with the territory of leading the research teams on finding a cure for the disease. One would have to be compassionate to be as dedicated as she was to the task.

That dedication was one of her more alluring traits.

I respected her need to fix the problem.

And something told me she'd never stop searching for a cure, even if it proved impossible. Riley wasn't one to give up easily, yet another attribute I admired about her.

However, that dedication to her cause meant I needed to approach this strategically.

Because wounding the Infected unnecessarily would bother her, as evidenced by the way she'd locked up outside of the compound earlier. I'd practically had to drag her to the plane.

I wouldn't be able to do that now—she was small, but not small enough to be carried around in my mouth like some pup.

Which meant not slaughtering the Infected with my jaws and claws.

Not exactly ideal, but I wanted Riley to cooperate, not freeze in the middle of a disease-ridden nest.

"All right," I said. "We're going to go through that line over there." I gestured toward the weakest section of the crowd. "Then we're going to run as fast as we can around the masses."

I locked gazes with her, wanting to be sure she'd heard the command in my tone. There would be no deviating from this plan.

Her bright blue eyes had darkened to a midnight shade in her wolf form—something I'd never seen before because she'd always ignored my offers to go for a run.

The dark orbs seemed to glow against her reddish-brown fur, the shade reminiscent of her auburn hair.

She was small for a Beta.

Almost frail.

Which had me a bit concerned about her ability to keep up, but she'd seemed to take offense to my questioning her shift a few minutes ago.

It was only natural after witnessing her change. The slowness of it had suggested she wasn't very experienced in shifting. Although, that couldn't be true because she was at least thirty years old.

However, something had definitely been off about it. I just didn't know what it was, and I really hoped it wouldn't slow us down now.

"I'm going to try to be as gentle with them as I can," I continued, telling her the full plan in hopes that it would make her more acquiescent to comply. "But we're severely outnumbered, Riley. And it's my job to protect you. Please remember that, okay?"

She snorted.

I wasn't sure if that was a scoffing sound or one of agreement, but I chose to assume it was the latter.

If she wanted to survive, then she needed to trust me.

And I was done submitting to this fiery little redhead.

I had been assigned to guard her for a reason, and I took my job very seriously. As should she.

Some respect would be appreciated, I thought at her.

But I didn't bother voicing it aloud. She'd made it clear from the beginning that she didn't approve of my role.

I had no idea why.

And I wasn't going to waste time now torturing myself by analyzing something only she could explain.

I rolled my neck, loosening my limbs, and gave my inner beast permission to take over. He eagerly agreed, shifting me to all fours in a graceful movement honed by almost a century of practice.

Much faster than Riley.

I was much bigger, too.

Something that became even more acutely evident as I stretched out beside her, preparing for our run.

Riley's wolf openly appraised mine, her dark irises roaming over every inch of my light-colored coat.

My animal practically preened beneath her perusal, the beast starved for her admiration after spending so many months pining for her like some teenage pup.

Ridiculous.

I wasn't sure what it was about this woman, but she constantly starred in my dreams.

And my darker fantasies, too.

Not the time, I told myself. *Focus on running. We can play later.*

I started forward at a trot, my ears attuned to Riley and the way her paws lightly brushed the concrete as she moved. *Lithe and delicate.*

Yet the female inside was all teeth. At least when it came to me.

Maybe this journey would be good for us—a way for her to realize I wasn't her enemy. A way for me to figure out the source of her behavior. *A way for me to prove my worth.*

Worth for what, I wasn't sure. But I wanted her to find me deserving of a chance.

It seemed like I'd spent the better part of the last few months trying to prove a point to her, only to be shot down at every turn.

Well, she couldn't avoid me now.

She needed me.

And I intended to demonstrate my strengths in the only way I knew how—by leading.

The Infected around us ambled slowly in our direction, their lack of coordination confirming that they hadn't fed recently. Most Infected maintained some form of natural instinct, which made some more dangerous than others.

But these beings weren't former military. There were no guns or weapons of any kind. Just teeth.

And my teeth were bigger.

My mental faculties were fully in check as well.

Riley stayed close to my side as we moved, putting my animal at ease as I scanned the perimeter again for another head count.

I started to slow when I realized there were more in this section than I'd originally noticed.

Shit.

There were *a lot* more.

They must have been hidden by the hill.

It didn't surprise me that there were so many Infected here. They'd probably chased a few meals to this location, as it was an obvious departure point.

But only if there was a plane available—of which ours appeared to be the only one in working order—and a pilot who knew how to fly.

I'd been around enough cockpits to know the basics. However, there were limits to my knowledge. And those limits included flying that jet to its final destination.

The only reason I'd even been able to land the damn thing here was because the pilot had set up some sort of path right before he'd turned.

Then the jet had gone sideways because his hand had jerked the steering. Once I'd righted it, I'd been able to put us back on track.

So he'd obviously been planning to land early and leave the jet.

Honorable, I supposed.

But he shouldn't have stepped onto the jet to begin with.

Fucking humans.

This was why I lacked sympathy for them—stupid decisions like not telling others about being bitten.

So many of them had this mentality of putting their own lives above everyone else's, even at the risk of others.

There were many supernaturals who now felt similarly, as many of us had chosen to favor our own survival by blocking the humans out. With how fast the disease mutated, it was crucial to isolate it to those already impacted by it.

But those decisions came after realizing the mortals were damning themselves beyond recognition.

And after some of the wolf clans had realized they were susceptible to the virus.

Right, I thought, scanning the growing crowd again. *This isn't going to work.*

I paused to reevaluate and noticed another potential weak link in the encircling group.

I started toward it, then stopped again as my nose picked up the strong scent of wrongness.

The fur along my spine danced in anticipation, my wolf ready to brawl.

I'd wanted to make this easy for Riley. But her safety and protection mattered more right now.

Which meant I was going to have to be a little less gentle than originally stated.

My wolf was fully on board.

I hoped Riley would be, too.

With a low warning growl, I took off back in the direction I'd originally indicated, and headed straight for the Infected.

Their excited screeches reminded me of nails on a chalkboard, drizzling ice through my veins.

I fucking hated that sound almost as much as their stench.

My wolf charged forward, ready for battle. But rather than slash at the Infected, I ran through them, knocking them down and creating a path for Riley to follow.

She did.

Or she tried to, anyway.

The Infected were so starved that they immediately converged on the gap, landing on top of her and trying to sink their teeth into her fur.

She released a ferocious little snarl and bit back, shocking the hell out of me.

When one of the Infected snagged her leg, she yelped and sank her fangs into his neck.

Her animal has taken control, I realized. Either Riley had willingly given the beast the reins, or the wolf had taken them out of a need to survive.

Regardless, I took advantage of the change and slashed out with my claws to help free her from the masses. Then I turned on another approaching horde and took several down with violent swipes of my paws.

Riley joined me, her snout sprinkled with drops of blood.

I grunted, telling her to follow me again, and took off through another crowd.

This one went down easily as both our wolves worked in tandem to create a safe path.

I stand corrected, I thought as we broke through the final mass. *This was easier than using a gun.*

But there wasn't time to do a victory lap because more Infected were already heading toward us.

I glanced back at the airport to acquaint myself with our surroundings and find my sense of direction again.

Riley growled, drawing my attention to her. She was staring down another pack of Infected, her teeth bared.

Definitely her wolf, I mused. Perhaps that was where all that feisty energy came from.

I nipped at her to grab her attention, then angled my head in the direction I wanted to run.

She blinked at me, as though coming out of a daze, her gaze running over my form once more. A little whine fell from her mouth, confusing me.

It was a distinctly submissive sound.

Betas and Omegas both bowed to Alphas on instinct, but something about that noise piqued my animal's interest. It'd almost resembled a plea.

For what? To run? To help her escape? To help her human regain control?

I wasn't sure.

Her dark orbs shone beneath the early morning sun, providing me with a glimpse of the human beneath the fur. There and gone in a second. She seemed to be fighting her animal.

So perhaps that was what she needed my help with— harnessing her beast.

Isn't that something she should already know how to do? I wondered. *That's what pups learn at the age of five.*

Regardless, there wasn't time to debate it or help her now. We needed to go.

I released a low purr, similar to what I'd done on the plane, the vibration instinctual and yet so incredibly wrong. Alphas purred for their intended mates or pack members who required it. And Riley certainly wasn't my intended, nor was she even a pack member.

Yet my wolf seemed to feel differently.

Considering the way her animal swayed toward mine, it seemed she appreciated the attention as well.

So I increased the volume to lull her into a state of obedience and led her around the incoming horde and into the tree line beside us.

We had to do a partial circle to go in the right direction, but there were far fewer Infected beneath the tree cover.

I avoided the few who stepped into our path, my purr never faltering, and took Riley deeper into the forest.

Her wolf followed mine as though entranced. She'd probably never heard an Alpha purr before. Some Alphas purred to help out fellow packmates, but Riley struck me as the kind of wolf who rarely needed that kind of soothing.

However, she seemed to respond positively to it.

Maybe this is the way to the little hellion's heart.

If it made her obedient, I'd purr for her every damn day.

I'd just chalk it up as a protection requirement.

We ran for several miles, our pace a quick trot that took us deeper and deeper into the woods.

Riley didn't fight me. She didn't growl. She didn't even try to slow down or alter our journey.

She just followed.

So you can obey commands, I mused. *You just need a little affection to do so.*

Or maybe this was why she'd denied my offers to go for a run in the past—she knew her wolf would submit to mine.

Fascinating.

I possessed the ability to force her to shift. Maybe I'd use that the next time she acted out.

I nearly snorted at the notion. Purring was a kinder alternative. I'd try that approach first. But I would definitely be noting her animal's easy acquiescence for future reference.

We continued our trek for a few hours, only stopping every now and then to sniff the wind and glance upward to check the sun.

I'd spent a lot of time outdoors, not only as a wolf but also as a man. I enjoyed losing myself in the wilderness and finding my way home. There was just something freeing about it. I'd never been much of a pack creature, preferring to roam on my own.

Maybe because I'd been raised with V-Clan wolves in Blood Sector. I'd always been an outcast as an X-Clan Alpha. But my Omega mother had fallen for a V-Clan Alpha, and as my biological father was dead, it made sense for us to live in Iceland with her mate's pack.

They were certainly different from most X-Clan packs that I knew. And not just because of their magical traits, but in the way they treated the members of their clans.

That could just be Blood Sector, though. As much as I didn't care for Kieran, he was a good leader. And he'd certainly won over the pack, despite his unique circumstances.

He'd won over Riley, too.

But that was another topic entirely, one my wolf didn't want to acknowledge right now. Because it was clear the two doctors were *close*.

I just didn't want to think about how *close* they were.

Or how she was always sweet to him. How she smiled for him. How she laughed for him.

And that's why I'm not going to think about it, I decided, picking up my pace a little.

Riley made a sound of protest, causing me to slow again and glance at her. It was her first outward sign of disobedience since we'd begun this trot, and looking at her now, I realized it wasn't her acting out. It was her saying she couldn't keep going.

Fuck.

I'd been so focused on our direction and surroundings that I hadn't noticed her exhausted state.

When was the last time you ate? I wondered, observing her frail form and pained eyes. *And why didn't you say something?*

Stubborn female.

She appeared ready to pass out.

Blaming her wasn't entirely fair, though. I should have been paying better attention to her.

Right. I sniffed the air, searching for signs of life anywhere around us. Or food. Maybe even water.

But instead, I caught a sweet fragrance on the wind.

Riley.

Odd. Her scent had always appealed to me. However, something was different about it now.

I inhaled again, trying to discern the distinctive note, but Riley shuddered, distracting me. We needed to find shelter and food.

With a reassuring purr, I angled my body toward the scent of freshly cut wood. That indicated human tampering, which meant it would lead us to something. Maybe a campsite or a cabin.

It turned out to be the latter.

Although, there wasn't just one cabin. There were several.

I paused near the trees and shifted back into human form so I could use my voice. My body shook from the sudden change, my neck cracking as my limbs straightened.

Riley stared up at me with glittering eyes, her wolf openly appraising me again.

"I'm going to go have a look around. Stay in animal form in case you need to run, okay?" I tried underlining my words with a little purr, hoping it would make her cooperate again.

Her wolf responded by sitting down on her rump.

Beautiful, I thought, fighting the urge to smile. "I'll howl if I find anything disturbing," I said instead, not wanting to risk her reverting back to her usual bratty state.

Then I took off on my bare feet toward the cabins, while fully engaging my shifter abilities along the way.

Time to hunt.

CHAPTER 4
RILEY

*S*tand up, I demanded.

My wolf lay down instead.

Look, I get it. You're mad that I didn't let you shift for, well, a while. But you have got to get it together.

My wolf huffed in reply and put her head on the ground, obedient to a fault. The Alpha had told her to "stay." So she was staying.

He's not our mate, I told her.

She snorted at that.

He's not ours, I repeated, the words ones I'd been chanting for hours. But she was utterly hypnotized by Jonas's purr.

Which, yeah, it was a nice purr. And I'd never actually been the recipient of an Alpha's purr before, so I'd rather enjoyed the way it'd made me feel.

However, that didn't mean I wanted to sit here like an obedient dog waiting for my master to return.

Unfortunately, that was *exactly* what my wolf wanted.

Hell, she wanted a lot more than that. She wanted Jonas's wolf to mount her.

Which was not happening.

The minute he realized I was an Omega, he'd claim me. I could feel the assurance of that all the way to my soul.

Just as I could sense my wolf's eager acceptance. *Worthy mate*, she practically purred. *My mate.*

He's not ours, I snapped again.

Which was a useless phrase, as my animal didn't truly understand my words or comments. She could sense my feelings, and usually we were in sync, but I'd more or less disassociated with her over the years because of the suppressants.

Suppressants that are quickly running out, I thought, sighing inside.

The cramps had begun a few miles back, which had eventually caused me to whimper a little. Because it *hurt*. It always did. And this heat would be worse than usual after years of blocking it from happening.

Fuck. I really needed to take charge and hide. Do something other than sit here like an obedient little Omega.

But I could sense my wolf's stubbornness.

She was part of me, after all. And I'd been born stubborn.

Hence the reason I'd chosen to leave my pack, attend a human university, and pursue all my degrees. My parents hadn't approved. They'd wanted me to settle down in Alberta Sector with the triad my father had chosen for me.

I'd run instead.

Something my father had tried to stop, but it had been easy to disappear among the humans during that time period. I'd been able to create a whole new identity, thanks to advanced technology, and apply to colleges.

Wolves stopped aging after a certain year, which allowed me to appear forever young.

Not that I'd been very old when I'd run.

Only nineteen and the perfect age to attend a university.

I'd acquired a lot of debt, but it'd been worth it to live my dreams.

My undergraduate in biology had led me to a medical degree. I'd gone through all the hoops of my residency, then furthered my studies by focusing on infectious diseases before finally acquiring a doctorate in epidemiology.

It'd been over a decade of school and practicing medicine.

But it had led me to my job at the CDC.

A job that had quickly turned into a nightmare when the brain-eating amoeba had mutated into its current state.

All it had taken was a group of teens visiting the wrong pond. They'd gone skinny-dipping and inhaled some water through their noses, and the disease had mutated from there.

Many politicians had called it a fluke.

Researchers had called it a perfect storm of events. Because the condition had mutated due to the unique subset already existent within its host.

I sighed inside. Now the disease had mutated beyond repair.

And the compound had been one of the only places with tissues for us to examine.

Did Kieran pack them? Or were they left to be destroyed?

Where are we even going, anyway? I wondered. Jonas hadn't actually told me. I'd just followed him blindly through the woods.

Well, no. My *wolf* had followed him blindly.

So what now?

Did I just sit here and wait to go into heat?

My stomach clenched at the notion.

Ugh.

It didn't help that I now knew exactly what I was working with. *The man has the body of a god.*

All lean lines. Muscular planes. Lickable abs. And a knot I very much wanted to acquaint myself with.

Don't think about it. Don't think about it. Don't think about it.

Oh, but I was absolutely thinking about it. That thick girth. His impressive package. Those heavy—

Stop, I snapped at myself. *He's not ours.*

My wolf huffed again, irritated by my denial. She'd wanted him for months and felt certain we were finally going to have him.

And that knot.

Inside me.

Securing us together.

In blissful agony.

I clenched my jaw. Or I tried to, anyway. But my wolf refused the action.

I could take back control, force her to heel, and shift back into human form. However, I was a bit concerned about how that would impact my impending heat. It was obviously already altering my mental faculties—hence the very beautiful image of a naked Jonas still gracing my thoughts—and shifting might worsen my current state.

A low whimper left my mouth again, the moan one I couldn't quite hold back.

It'd been so long since I'd indulged in sex. I'd been with a few Betas, as well as a few humans. But never an Alpha. For obvious reasons. I didn't want to be claimed against my will.

However, the more I considered Jonas, the more I wouldn't mind him claiming me.

Which scared the shit out of me because I knew that was my heat talking, not my mind.

Not ours. Not ours. Not ours.

Think about what he'll do when he finds out the truth, I thought. *Think about how angry he'll be.*

I'd defied the value of being an Omega by taking suppressants. As an Alpha, he would be furious with me. He'd probably punish me by refusing to knot me.

At least for a period of time.

Long enough to make me beg.

Really beg.

A low growl formed inside me at the thought. *I hate him. I hate Alphas. I hate* this.

But mostly, I hated that I wanted Jonas.

This would be much easier if I truly hated the man. Alas, he hadn't done anything to warrant my hatred.

Other than exist, anyway.

I released a long sigh, this one trailing through my wolf. She was the epitome of calm, her ears perked and listening for Jonas's return.

No thoughts regarding our survival.

No thoughts of running.

Just a quiet acceptance of fate.

This is why the human side is given more control, I told her. *We have common sense. You just think with your reproductive system.*

She snorted, not because she understood me necessarily, just my tone. Or perhaps my disgruntled reaction to her relaxation.

We weren't completely disconnected, just enough for her to have control right now.

Something I wondered if Jonas had facilitated by his movements and words and *purr.*

No, probably not. It was my fault for denying my wolf all these years.

Now that I'd set her free, she wanted to be in charge.

And her first matter of business seemed to be accepting Jonas as a mate.

He doesn't even know you're an Omega. He thinks you're just a Beta.

Another grunt.

He doesn't want us.

She ignored that.

She ignored *me*.

Likely because she knew I was full of shit. He absolutely wanted us. Or he would the moment he realized the truth.

How will he punish me? I wondered, my insides tingling at the prospect. *Orgasm denial? A spanking? Harsh growling?*

Why did all those things appeal to me?

Oh, right. Because my body had a mind of its own.

Why didn't I just take my suppressants earlier? I had to go question everything. Of course, it was a good thing I hadn't taken them, or I wouldn't have been able to shift and run with Jonas. So he would have found out something was wrong anyway.

And that would have been even worse.

Maybe.

Or maybe this will be worse because now I'm going to want his knot.

With the suppressants, I could deny him.

In this state, I couldn't. Because all my forbidden desires were coming out to play.

My wolf's nose twitched as Jonas's scent grew stronger. But there was something tainting his woodsy cologne. Something smoky.

I sat up. Or rather, my *wolf* sat up.

But neither of us liked the scent.

What is that? Why has he altered his natural state?

We sniffed the air, our nose curling.

Not acceptable.

Jonas came into view half a beat later wearing a pair of jeans and boots.

Also not acceptable, I thought. *Why are you dressed?*

Wait. Why do I want him naked?

Stop. Thinking.

He held up some fabric. "I found you a sundress. It's pink."

Yes. I have eyes, I replied with a look. *I can see the color.*

"I found a cabin with some canned food, linens, and a few other items. Including a bed. So we can rest there." He glanced around, his nostrils flaring. "There are no signs of any Infected nearby. No humans, either." His brow furrowed. "But there's something..." He trailed off as his nose crinkled. "What is that? It smells..."

My wolf started wagging her tail.

Her *fucking* tail.

This is not a good thing, I told her. *This is a bad thing.*

As evidenced by the way his icy gaze immediately found mine, his nostrils flaring again. "*Sweet.*"

It took me a moment to understand what he meant.

Then I realized he was finishing his sentence. *It smells sweet.*

Yeah, because it's me going into heat.

"Riley..." He took a step forward, the pink fabric fluttering to the ground beside him. "Why do you smell like an Omega?"

Shit.

I stood up, my wolf suddenly relinquishing control back to me.

Maybe because she could sense the aggression pulsing

48

around him, that Alpha anger I'd anticipated upon him realizing *why* my scent had started to change.

I was honestly shocked that he hadn't realized it while we'd been running.

However, the cramping had only started a little bit ago. Which meant the final vestiges of my suppressants had probably just started to metabolize. So my scent had only recently begun to shift.

Even now, I could still smell some of the sour notes of my forced Beta perfume.

But Jonas was right—my Omega sweetness was definitely taking over.

He moved forward again, and I backed up on instinct.

"Don't you dare run," he growled. "Shift back and explain this to me. Right fucking now."

My wolf whined, wanting to agree.

However, she'd given me back the control I needed to make the decisions between us.

Which meant I was absolutely going with option one —*running*.

And he knew it, too. His Alpha snarl grew, the sound one that would force my shift if I didn't react immediately.

So I took off into the woods, not back the way we'd come, but sideways to… I had no idea where.

I didn't care.

I just knew I had to run.

To escape.

To *hide*.

Because I refused to be claimed. I wanted my dreams, my life, my *choice*.

And Jonas wouldn't give that to me.

He'd take me. Mount me. Knot me. Impregnate me. And *own* me.

Not. Happening.

My wolf appeared to be completely on board now, allowing me to push myself to my limits as we rushed through the underbrush.

Except a note of excitement wafted around her spirit, giving me pause.

Why are you enjoying this? I wondered. *We're literally about to face the biggest battle of our life. And you're* panting?

Fuck, the damn wolf was *smiling*.

It wasn't an exhausted pant, but a happy one.

Because she could sense Jonas chasing us.

She knew her chosen Alpha was on the hunt.

And my damn animal *wanted* to be caught.

This was her version of a mating game.

Oh, fuck me, I thought. *This is not going to end well.*

CHAPTER 5
JONAS

SOMEWHERE IN NORTH CAROLINA

R*iley's an Omega.*

And not just any Omega, but an Omega going into heat.

Her sweet perfume called to my wolf, forcing me to trail after her along the forest floor. I'd accidentally given her a bit of a head start, mostly because I'd been too busy gaping after her fleeing form to immediately react.

Then I'd kicked off my boots and ripped off my borrowed pants, shifted to all fours, and took off through the woods.

What. The. Fuck?

How had I missed this crucial detail? My wolf had craved the female for months. I'd thought it was the aspect of a challenge that had intrigued him.

But no.

He'd suspected her true form all along.

And it seemed I now had an answer as to why she'd refused to run with me.

51

Because her petite wolf was all Omega. That explained the size and her instinct to obey.

Her animal was inherently submissive.

While the woman beneath the fur was all feisty female.

A feisty female who had clearly been taking suppressants.

But why? Why hide her natural form? To avoid her heat? There were other ways to seek comfort during estrus, ways that didn't require drugging her wolf.

She should know better. She was a doctor, for crying out loud.

At least that meant she'd probably been safe about it.

Of course, if a simple shift sent her back into Omega mode, then was it really safe at all?

Fuck, was *that* why she'd hesitated about shifting earlier? When was the last time she'd gone for a run?

No wonder her transition had been slow.

I'd been right to be concerned. And then I'd made her run for hours.

Fuck.

Had she said something, I wouldn't have pushed her so hard. This all explained her exhaustion, too. She also likely hadn't eaten today.

Damn it, Riley, I thought, my paws pounding across the ground as I pursued her.

She was out there pushing her limits yet again. Right as she was about to go into heat, too.

This female must possess a death wish. Because she was going to end up severely injured, or worse, at this rate.

What we needed to do was go back to the little cabin village and create a protective den for her to rest in throughout her cycle.

Would it be impacted by her suppressants? When was the last time she'd even gone into estrus?

I had so many fucking questions, and there was only one wolf out there who could answer them. A wolf whose scent had just diminished to a faint perfume.

My wolf sniffed, confused.

Then he cocked his head, his ears attuned to all the sounds of the forest.

And the gentle flow of running water in the distance.

Clever female, I thought, picking up speed again. She must have entered the stream to help wash off her scent.

Too bad for her, it wouldn't be enough.

I followed the sound of water rolling over rocks, found a creek not far from where I'd lost her scent, and scanned the darkening forest. The sun was low in the sky, indicating the early evening hour.

Which meant we'd run for probably nine or ten hours today.

Riley had to be exhausted, especially if she was going into heat.

I needed to find her before she truly injured herself. Omegas weren't necessarily fragile; they were just small. But Riley hadn't been taking proper care of her wolf. That much had been evident by her shift alone.

I just hadn't realized the extent of the damage until her scent had changed.

Fucking suppressants.

At least it answered a lot of questions.

Although, it inspired several more.

Come out, come out, wherever you are, I thought, scanning the area by the water's edge.

My wolf could sense her nearby. She hadn't continued moving. She'd stayed by the water, perhaps even in it, to mask her scent.

Which meant she was hiding somewhere.

Such a smart little wolf, I mused. My beast seemed pleased as well, his instincts inspired by the hunt.

He saw this as a test. A way to prove his worth as a potential mate.

Our animals never allowed emotions or external factors to play into a decision. When my wolf wanted something, he took it.

And right now, he wanted Riley.

I wouldn't let him outright claim her, but I'd give him some freedom to seduce her wolf.

Then I'd purr for her when she accepted my beast.

Assuming Riley's penchant for disobedience didn't interfere with the courting ritual.

It's Riley. Of course she'll rebel.

I almost snorted.

But then another thought occurred to me.

One that soured my stomach.

Is this why she's always been rude to me? Because I'm an X-Clan Alpha? Has it all been her way of telling me she doesn't consider me worthy of her?

My wolf snorted in disagreement, clearly aware of the doubt trickling through my mind. He didn't doubt a damn thing. He could smell the interest coming from her animal.

She wants us, he was saying. *Now let's find her and knot her.*

I gave him the reins, allowing him to drive the hunt.

If Riley found me unworthy, it was because she hadn't given me a chance to prove myself. So I'd let my wolf do the speaking for me through actions rather than words.

I'd never actively pursued a mate before. I'd been too busy acting as an enforcer for hire. Which had eventually led me to my position as Riley's guard.

Was it fate? Maybe.

Or just a happenstance of our paths crossing.

Regardless, we would be discussing a future. Even if

that future simply included me helping her through this estrus. Because she would need a knot soon and mine was the only one readily available.

No Kieran here to play with, little one, I thought, satisfied. Because I'd seen their little flirtatious smiles and the way he'd made her laugh.

Fucking Alpha Prince.

That title didn't make him royalty. It was just a formal designation the V-Clan wolves used for their Sector Alpha positions.

I could be a Sector Alpha for an X-Clan pack. I was old enough. Strong enough. Fast enough. *Smart* enough.

But I'd never attempted to join a sector or a clan because I preferred my calling as an enforcer.

If Riley wanted a *prince*, then maybe Kieran was the better choice. He certainly had the arrogance of a royal.

Thinking about Kieran and how Riley might prefer his knot to mine made my wolf growl, his irritation both at me and at the Omega hiding from him.

Doubt was an emotion my beast refused to entertain. He felt certain of his pursuit.

It was the man in me that questioned everything because of Riley's bizarre behavior.

Which was really fucking annoying because I didn't question things. Ever. But that woman left me conflicted about every damn decision in her presence due to her bratty behavior.

All because she's been hiding her Omega status.

That was the heart of it all—she just didn't want me to find out.

Well, I know now. And I'm going to find you.

She was nearby. I could feel her presence. Her heat. Her *need*. The scent of it wrapped around me like a drugging cloak, drawing me farther upstream.

My wolf slowed, his focus falling to a set of bigger rocks along the edge. The kind of rock formation that a small wolf could hide within.

He prowled up on top of the rocks and lay down.

Then growled.

A soft little whimper came from beneath the stones. *Riley.*

Another rumble left my chest, causing her to slowly slip out into the water.

Her eyes met mine.

I knew when her body jerked that she was about to run, and my wolf reacted before she could take more than a step.

We *pounced.*

Rolled.

Snarled.

And pinned our Omega to the water's edge.

She shivered beneath us, another of those whines leaving her snout.

You're ours now, little one, I thought at her, my wolf growling once more, this time in warning. *Shift or I'll make you shift.*

She exposed her throat, her belly already touching mine.

And began to transition back into human form.

I balanced myself above her with my paws on either side of her head, not wanting to risk hurting her or smothering her with my weight. The rocks beneath her neck and shoulders were probably sharp and uncomfortable. I would have tackled her in the grass, but the stream had made it easier to trap her.

Once she finished her change, I joined her, my human side overtaking my animal in half the time as hers. *Because I haven't been throttling my instincts with suppressants*, I muttered to myself.

Her bright blue eyes met mine again, a hint of fire lurking in their depths.

Here we go.

"Get off of me," she demanded. Yet her thighs spread to allow me to settle between them. Because yeah, her body wanted me—as evidenced by the slickness now coating my groin. Slickness that had nothing to do with the shallow water beneath her legs.

I ignored her command and issued one of my own. "Start. Talking."

It was an order that shouldn't be very hard for Riley to follow, as the woman usually had no problem speaking her mind.

Yet now, of all times, she chose to remain silent.

And mutinously glare up at me.

While simultaneously pressing up into my cock with an obvious invitation to fuck.

It was an invitation I would accept *after* we discussed her antics.

"Riley," I growled, ensuring she understood that I wasn't in the mood to be denied. Not with her sweet and *wet* body beneath me. "I'm about five seconds away from knotting you, *Omega*. Explain to me how that's even possible."

I already knew the cause—*suppressants*.

What I really wanted was for her to explain *why*.

She swallowed, some of the fire dying in her gaze.

I narrowed my eyes. "Answer me. Tell me why you took suppressants." Maybe informing her of what I obviously knew already would help her open up.

"I… I wanted a life…" The soft words weren't the ones I'd expected to hear, causing me to frown. I'd never heard her speak in that tone before. It made her that much more *Omega*.

And I wasn't sure if I liked it.

Riley was all feisty prowess, which I admired about her.

I didn't want her meek and submissive. I simply wanted *her*.

"I wanted to *live*," she continued with a little more power, some part of her seeming to snap into place again. "To be more than a pup-maker."

My eyebrows flew upward. "More than a *what*?"

"You heard me," she replied, her blue eyes gleaming with liquid fire once more.

There's my girl, I thought. *Keep talking.*

"I'm more than just my designation. But all you Alphas ever see is an Omega you can knot. And I wanted *more*."

Well, *that* made me growl. "I see a lot more than an Omega I can knot," I informed her.

"Oh yeah?" She pressed up against me, her slick center coating my cock in hot arousal. "Weren't you five seconds away from knotting me, *Alpha*?"

"You're going into heat." I couldn't keep the rumble out of my voice. "So yeah, I'm going to knot you."

"Without any regard for my desires?"

"Are you refusing me?" I countered, playing her at her own game and shifting my hips in a way that allowed me to rub her needy little clit. "Do you want to go into heat alone?"

"Why do you think I ran away?" she tossed back.

"Because your wolf wanted to test mine." I moved against her again, loving the way her nipples beaded against my chest in response. "And now she knows with certainty that I'm a worthy mate. Which is why you're practically panting beneath me, Riley. You want my knot."

She growled in response. "I'm going into heat after over a decade without sex. I'd take any knot right now."

My eyes narrowed. "Any knot?"

"That's what I said, Alpha. I'm an Omega. Any knot will do. So yeah, I'm reacting to yours."

I went back to my knees between her spread legs, taken aback by her callous statement.

I'd been craving this female for months.

Yet she'd essentially just said, *I suppose you'll do since I have no other choice.*

After everything I'd done for her. Protecting her. Choosing her life over mine. Putting *her* first every step of the way.

And she thanks me by insinuating that she is only reacting to my knot because she's going into heat and I'm the only one available?

Fuck. That.

I'd passed her wolf's test. I'd proved my skill set and worth for *months.*

If she didn't find me worthy enough for more than just my knot, then I wasn't about to give it to her.

"Fine." I pushed away from her and stood.

Which, of course, drew her gaze to my throbbing dick.

But fuck if I was going to offer it to her now. Not after *that* insult.

Any knot.

"I'll make you a safe place in the cabin for your heat. Or you can stay out here and fend for yourself." I wasn't going to tie her to a bed and force her to take my knot.

I wasn't that kind of Alpha.

Some would have just taken her and demanded her supplication. But I wanted my female warm and willing, not *settling.*

Perhaps that was my V-Clan influence. Because my father certainly hadn't been that way with my mother. He, along with three others, had taken her during one of her heats. Then they'd brawled for the chance to mate her.

Which had led to his death.

And my mother being saved by her current mate.

So yeah, taking an Omega against her will was a bit of a hot button for me, considering that was how I'd essentially been created.

This was all something Riley would know if she'd actually tried talking to me.

But no. She'd refused me for reasons I didn't understand.

And right now, I wasn't sure I even wanted to know.

Any knot.

Yeah.

Good luck with that, Doctor.

"Have fun in the woods," I said and started back on foot toward the cabins.

There weren't any threats out here right now. Riley would be fine. And if she chose to go deeper into the forest, then I'd track her down and stay nearby to protect her.

Because that was my job.

But once I got her to the base, I was putting in for a transfer.

Because fuck this.

And fuck her.

CHAPTER 6
RILEY

Somewhere in North Carolina

*W*ait, *that's it?*

I frowned.

Then I dipped my head back to see that Jonas had left, his steps silent.

What the hell?

I sat up, wet from the damn stream and other things.

He fucking left.

My wolf growled inside me, furious.

But she wasn't mad at him. She was mad at me.

She might not have understood words, but she understood that I'd insulted her chosen Alpha. *"I'd take any knot right now."*

Okay. That wasn't fair. Nor was it true. I would eventually reach that state while in estrus, which was why I hated going into heat, but I wasn't near that point yet. I could easily choose right now.

And yeah, I'd choose him over all the Alphas I knew.

I'd just been pissed at the situation. Pissed that he'd caught me. Pissed that I'd *liked* how he'd caught me. Pissed with how easily I was giving in to him. Pissed that we were in the middle of the woods, away from my labs, and nowhere near my suppressants.

Pissed that some part of me was thankful for all of the above.

Thankful that it was Jonas and no one else.

Thankful that we were *alone*.

I'm so fucked up, I thought, curling into a ball on my side as a pang hit my lower abdomen. *What am I even doing?*

And what is he doing?

He'd just left me here.

What kind of Alpha left an Omega alone when she was about to go into heat? He should be fucking me already, bringing me that much closer to the edge of my impending insanity.

Not walking away.

Alphas didn't give Omegas choices. They took what they wanted.

Does he not want me?

My frown deepened. *No, he definitely wants me.* I'd seen the evidence of that hanging between his thick thighs.

He'd walked away out of pride because I'd insulted his knot. I'd insulted *him*.

Most Alphas would have just fucked me in response, told me to behave and take it and *enjoy*. Proved their prowess and the size of their knots through action alone.

Yet Jonas leaving me here proved a different sort of point.

I'd rejected him, and he'd more or less accepted it.

Which made him a very different kind of Alpha indeed.

"I'll make you a safe place in the cabin for your heat. Or you can stay out here and fend for yourself."

He hadn't said he would make *us* a safe place, only me. Because he was accepting my choice? Or because he was too angry with me to fuck me now?

Angry Alphas were typically terrifying, not reasonable. Yet he'd been all quiet fury, leaving me here without a single roar.

I sat up, my palm on my stomach as my insides rioted again. I did not miss this sensation.

Blowing out a breath, I tried to move up to my feet and swayed a little. *I'm good. I've got this.* I took a step, my toe catching on one of the stones.

A yelp left me as I crashed back into the stream, my palms just barely catching me before I fell headfirst into a damn rock.

"*Shit!* That fucking hurt!" My knee was definitely bleeding. And my toe ached from stumbling into the stone. I'd been much more graceful on four paws. But I couldn't shift again right now. I was too exhausted. Too hungry. Too *weak*.

Which just pissed me off even more.

I hated feeling weak. That was part of why I despised being an Omega. Part of what I couldn't stand about my *heat*. It left me vulnerable and needy, two traits forced upon me by birth.

I'd fought hard not to be either of those things.

Yet here I was, practically crawling to the water's edge because I couldn't even seem to stand.

My chin wobbled with the urge to cry, which just infuriated me more. And that led to tears blurring my vision.

I. Hate. Everything.

This whole crisis of self-pity wasn't me. Everything about this situation *wasn't me.*

Or maybe it was.

Maybe it was the very *me* that I'd been hiding from for over a decade.

I finally reached the water's edge and crawled up onto the grassy bank. *Get it together, Riley. You're stronger than this. You're better than this.*

But it was hard to feel *strong* and *better* when my insides were pulsing with *need.*

I should have just let Jonas fuck me, not insulted him and chased him off. Although, if I were being honest with myself, *chasing him off* hadn't been my intention at all. I'd wanted to infuriate him so that he would fuck me in anger. Which would have allowed me to hate him later.

However, he hadn't done that at all.

He'd completely left me instead, something no Alpha would ever have done in my former pack.

Jonas isn't like those Alphas, I reminded myself.

It was something I'd sort of suspected about him, as he'd always been quiet and observant rather than domineering and authoritative. He had his moments with the latter traits, but those only seemed to come out when he was in protective mode.

Never really *possessive* or cruel. Just a caring guard.

And I'd just insulted him in a way I'd never think to insult any other Alpha.

What the fuck is wrong with me?

I knew the answer to that. It was more rhetorical than anything. I pressed my forehead to the ground and sighed.

Get up, Riley.

Get up.

Walk back to the cabins.

Apologize.

And accept his offer for safety.

My arms shook as I forced myself up off the ground. A slight groan left my mouth when I finally found my footing, my shins and knees screaming at me for scraping them up so badly.

And that groan turned into a sharp gasp when I found Jonas leaning against a tree, watching me.

Naked.

Of course he was naked. He'd been naked on top of me, like, five minutes ago. I was still naked, too.

But he didn't seem to be interested in my nudity. His gaze was on my legs, taking in my battle wounds from the stream.

He was still aroused—as was I—however, he made no move to walk toward me.

"Have you decided to stay here or go back to the cabin?" he asked, his tone giving nothing away.

"C-cabin," I stammered.

He nodded. "Good choice."

He pushed off the tree, but rather than come toward me, he started in the direction of the cabin.

I frowned at his back. He'd definitely been gone when I'd looked up before. Had he returned when he'd heard me fall? Why hadn't he helped me out of the stream?

Probably because he thought I'd deserved that trip over my own feet.

Which, yeah, after the way I'd spoken to him, I probably had.

Actually, I probably deserved a lot worse for the way I'd treated him thus far. I'd never been particularly kind to him. But it wasn't because I disliked him. I just... I didn't want him to know about me being an Omega because I knew he'd take away my choice and claim me.

Although, he'd proved me wrong when he'd walked away without a backward glance.

Except then he'd returned... just to leave me again.

This time, I started after him, his name on my tongue.

Only for my fucking toe to get snagged on a tree root.

My palms immediately moved to protect my upper body, but they didn't reach the ground. They landed against Jonas's hips instead as he caught me.

With my face nearly meeting his groin.

I jumped backward, only to hit the same damn root.

Jonas grabbed my waist and pulled me against him, his eyebrows flying upward. "Have you forgotten how to properly move on two feet, Doctor?"

I huffed out a breath. "Apparently."

"Hmm," he hummed. "Then maybe you should shift."

"I can't," I mumbled. "It'll use up the rest of my energy and probably send me into an immediate heat."

He stared down at me for a long minute. "Do you need me to carry you?" His tone suggested it was the last thing he wanted to do.

Which, of course, had me wanting to agree just to piss him off.

However, I swallowed the urge and shook my head. "I can walk. Just... slowly."

He studied me for another beat, then released me.

I nearly tripped a third time—*or was it a fourth?*—but my foot met the ground this time, holding me steady.

Jonas arched an inquisitive brow.

"I'm exhausted, okay?" I admitted. "And obviously lacking in coordination."

"I offered to carry you."

"In a tone that clearly indicated how much you didn't want to do that," I replied. "So no. I'll walk."

"Why do you always have to be so difficult?" he

demanded. "I'm trying to help you, Dr. Campbell."

I winced at his formal address.

Dr. Campbell.

Not Riley.

"*Fuck.* All I've ever done is help you," he continued. "Yet you fight me at every turn. Why? Is it because you didn't want a guard? Did you want to handle all this on your own? Or am I a special case? Because I certainly don't see you acting like this around *Prince Kieran.*"

My eyes widened a little at the venom in his tone when he said Kieran's name.

But it was really his whole speech that surprised me.

Because it was the second one he'd given me today.

Who knew the sexy Alpha bodyguard could be so talkative?

He continued to stare at me—well, no, he was *glaring* at me—while waiting for a reply.

When I didn't voice one, he just shook his head and started walking again.

"I declined because my first instinct was to accept," I called after him. "I was trying not to be 'difficult.'" I deepened my voice on that final word in an attempt to sound like Jonas.

He paused. "That doesn't make any sense."

"Well, I wanted to accept because I knew you didn't want to do it, which would be me being vindictive. So I said *no* in an attempt to be nice."

He turned around to face me, his long blond hair flowing in unruly waves around his handsome face. "Why not just tell me what you actually want without using it as an opportunity to be *nice* or *vindictive?*" he suggested.

I twisted my lips to the side, unable to really answer that. It was never truly about that between us. I just... I just wanted him to *leave.* He was a complication I didn't want to deal with, not while handling everything else.

But that wasn't exactly fair to him, which I knew. However, I doubted he would ever genuinely understand my immediate distrust of the situation.

I was an Omega.

He was an Alpha.

In his mind, I was a cherished wolf meant to carry his pups, or the pups of another Alpha. Nothing more. Nothing less.

He wouldn't understand my drive to be anything else. None of them did.

Jonas blew out a breath and drew his fingers through his hair. "Why can't you respect me like you do the others?" he asked, making me frown. "What have I done to earn your obvious dislike?"

"I don't dislike you," I started.

"Well, you obviously don't like me either," he countered. "So what's your problem? What do you need from me for us to get along?"

"I…" I wasn't sure how to answer that.

All my wolf wanted him to do was mount me. He was exuding a hell of a lot of dominance right now, which I supposed he always did, but there was something even more intense about his posture and tone now.

"You're about to go into heat in the middle of the fucking woods during an apocalypse," he said, a subtle growl underlining some of his words. "It's going to take a hell of a lot of effort to protect you through that."

A lump formed in my throat, making it difficult to swallow. "Depends on your version of protection."

He gave me a look that suggested my response was the wrong one.

"Protection being barricading the damn den, listening to you beg for a knot, and fighting off anything that responds to that screaming," he defined. "While also fighting the urge to suit your 'any knot will do' requirement."

I flinched. Yeah, I deserved that barb. But that didn't mean I liked it.

"And afterward, I have to escort you to the base."

"Which base?" I asked.

"Fort Bragg," he replied. "We only held a five-mile-an-hour pace today, so it's at least another two hundred miles from here. Likely more."

I was familiar with Fort Bragg.

But it wasn't a CDC facility.

I almost asked where we were going afterward, but Jonas wasn't done speaking.

"That means we have about two weeks together, Doctor. There's no one coming for us. No other Alpha to guard you. So tell me what you need to make this work, and I'll do it." He didn't sound defeated so much as exhausted. And not exhausted as in tired, just... tired of me. My antics. My rudeness.

Which he had every right to feel.

I'd been nothing but hostile toward him from the beginning.

"I don't dislike you," I said again.

He grunted but didn't say anything else. All he did was fold his arms across that chiseled chest and stare at me. *Waiting.*

"I didn't want you to find out what I am," I finally admitted. "You're an Alpha. You take. And I don't want to be taken."

Another grunt. "Is that what I'm doing right now, Doctor? Am I *taking*?"

"Well, no. Not yet. But—"

"You don't know a damn thing about me, Dr. Campbell. And you've never tried to know me." His arms fell to his sides as he stepped toward me. "If I wanted to fuck you, all I'd have to do is growl. I'd have you weeping on your knees in seconds."

I swallowed, part of me hoping he would prove his point by doing just that.

It would make this so much easier.

However, the ice coating his blue eyes told me it was the last thing he wanted to do right now. "There would be no *taking*, only *giving*," he added.

He stopped only a few feet away from me, his nostrils flaring.

I wasn't sure what to say to him. Because he was right. One growl and I'd be begging him to fuck me.

"I have always been professional with you because I take my job seriously," he said after an uncomfortable beat. "That isn't going to change now. Do you need me to carry you, Dr. Campbell?"

"Please stop calling me that," I said, hating the way the formality just seemed to roll off his tongue. It was almost an insult at this point.

"Answer the question, Doctor."

That wasn't any better.

However, his expression told me it wasn't up for debate.

I blew out a breath and decided he'd more than earned an honest response. "I haven't eaten today. My body is undergoing... *changes*. And I'm tired. So while I could walk, I would be much slower than you."

I hated admitting all that.

But it was true.

"And..." I paused, mentally preparing to voice the rest of my response. "And I don't think now is a good time for me to be stubborn. Therefore, I may not need to be carried, but I would like to be carried. Please."

CHAPTER 7
JONAS

That had to be the most civilized response Dr. Riley Campbell had ever given me.

"All right." I closed the gap between us. "Bridal-style or piggyback ride?"

She snorted.

I arched a brow. "Answer the question, Doctor."

She rolled her eyes and shook her head. "Bridal-style, *Alpha*. May as well pretend, right?"

"Pretend what?" I asked, picking her up while I spoke. We needed to get back so I could properly put the den together. And I'd rather do that before we completely lost the sun.

"That we're in love?" she suggested as I started walking. "That we're courting? That we're dating? Whatever it is we're supposed to do before you knot me for a week."

I grunted. "I'm not going to knot you, Omega."

She laughed. "Right."

I stopped and looked down at her. "You are aware that Alphas can control their rutting instincts, right?"

She gave me a look that told me she absolutely did not know that. "No Alpha wants to control their rut."

"I didn't say they want to, Doctor. I said they *can*." I resumed walking, my gaze going to our surroundings.

"I've never seen an Alpha control his urges. It's not possible."

"Well, you're about to see me control mine," I informed her flatly. The strongest of our kind possessed the ability to maintain control at all times, even when tested by a needy Omega.

She might not have realized it, but I was a strong Alpha. A *very* strong Alpha.

"I almost want to make a bet," she mused, proving her ignorance and essentially insulting me yet again.

Rather than point it out, I merely muttered, "It's one you would lose."

"So confident."

I didn't reply. She could pretend to know whatever she wanted. I'd prove her wrong through my actions, which meant more than words.

"Weren't you just saying how you were five seconds away from knotting me?" she asked after several minutes of silence.

"Weren't you just saying how you didn't want to be difficult?" I countered. "Yet you're goading me right now. Some would say that's being difficult, Doctor."

"Because you went from saying you were going to knot me in five seconds to saying you're not going to knot me at all. I'm just pointing out the contradiction, *Alpha*."

She kept throwing that title at me like it was an insult.

I'd been born an Alpha. I'd embraced it. Just because

she saw being an Omega as a weakness or something to hide didn't mean I felt the same way about my designation in life.

"You keep talking about controlling urges," she continued. "But you were ready to knot me in the stream."

"Yes. When I thought your wolf wanted mine," I replied, picking up the pace because I really wanted to end this conversation. And the only way to do that would be by depositing her in a cabin and locking her in a fucking room.

"And now?" she pressed, because clearly she didn't know when to stop. "You no longer want to knot me?" The teasing lilt in her tone had me clenching my jaw.

Is this all a game to her?

Or was she just trying to goad me into proving some sort of point by making me fuck her?

"What point are you trying to make here?" I asked her, tired of these word games. I didn't enjoy speaking on a good day. And today was far from good.

"That you wanted to knot me and that you're still going to want to knot me," she said. "I accept that because it's how our wolves work. So if you can't maintain control, I'll understand."

I grunted again. "I'll be fine." However, she wouldn't be. She'd be in pain, and it would hurt me not to help her, but I wouldn't be just *any knot* for her.

"Seriously, Jonas. I don't need you to prove your control to me. It's okay."

I stopped again to glare down at her, done with this fucking conversation. "This is about more than proving my control, Omega. You made it very clear that you don't want me. And that's fine. I accept your rejection. Which is why I won't be knotting you."

She blanched. "I didn't reject you."

I shook my head and started walking again. This had to be the longest mile in the history of miles.

"I didn't reject you," she repeated. "I just said I'm about to go into heat. I'll react to any knot. That's biology, Jonas."

"Right," I agreed. "Any knot." Not *my* knot. Even though her wolf had challenged mine and I'd won that challenge.

However, the female didn't see it that way.

She didn't want me. She didn't *know* me. She'd made it clear from the beginning of our working relationship that she wanted nothing to do with me.

I'd wanted to fuck it out of her. Although, now I didn't want my knot anywhere near her.

Because I refused to be *any knot*.

Maybe my ego had played a role in my decision, or perhaps my wounded wolf was the cause, but either way, I wasn't changing my mind.

Riley fell quiet for so long that I wondered if she'd passed out. But a glance downward showed me a beautiful face with wide blue eyes. She was staring at me in a way she'd never looked at me before. Like she'd finally realized I was a man.

I forced my gaze away from hers and focused on the woods again, needing to get her back to the cabin.

Her scent was sweetening with each passing second, her Omega genetics calling to the beast inside me. My instinct to claim her rode me hard, especially because of the little game her wolf had played with my animal.

I won, he kept saying. *Mine.*

Except the human half of the shifter didn't want us.

Her small hand suddenly stroked my chin, her fingertips grazing my stubbled jaw. I instinctively moved away from her touch, my wolf growling inside.

She flinched and pulled her hand back. "Sorry."

"Don't test my control," I gritted out through my clenched teeth. "You won't like the consequences." Not because I'd knot her, but because I would discipline her.

By locking her in a fucking room to suffer alone.

Which, arguably, I was already going to do, but I could at least try to help by purring for her. Assuming my animal even allowed it at this point.

"I'm not trying to test your control," she snapped back. "I just… I wanted to touch you."

"It's not your right to touch me, Doctor."

She released a disgruntled little growl of her own, causing my wolf to stand up and take notice. He rather liked that sound. "I didn't reject you, *Alpha*. But I'll concede that I *insulted* you."

All I could do was grunt in response. I wasn't having this conversation again.

"I didn't mean to insult you, Jonas."

Another statement unworthy of a response. Whether she meant to or not, she'd done it. *Repeatedly*. For months.

A year.

I'd tolerated it because I'd seen it as a challenge. Now I understood that it wasn't a challenge; it was an Omega rejecting an Alpha.

I would not be my biological father.

I would not force myself on an unwilling Omega.

I'd been raised by a good Alpha. He was a V-Clan wolf with a penchant for the night and a taste for blood, but he was also a strong man. An *honorable* Alpha.

He still protected my mother, living peacefully in Blood Sector.

Well, as peacefully as one could during this turbulent time.

But his safety and security were what had allowed me

to explore other options. To live outside of the nest. Otherwise, I would have felt compelled to remain home to protect my mother.

Neither of them had withheld the story of my birth, or the events that had led up to it.

He'd claimed my mother while I was still in her womb.

They hadn't known what it would do to me.

But I'd been all X-Clan Alpha.

Although, if Riley was to be believed, that meant I had no control. So hey, maybe I adopted that "power" from my mother's mate.

"You're really mad," Riley marveled. "I don't think I've seen you mad before."

It took physical restraint not to react to that asinine comment. Whether she was purposefully goading me or not, I really didn't know. It seemed all she did was try to piss me off. So why would now be any different?

She fell quiet again, giving me a few minutes of blissful silence.

Until she suddenly jolted against me.

I nearly dropped her as she wrapped her arms around my abdomen, a moan falling from her lips that sounded extremely pained.

Her eyes squeezed shut as she tried to breathe through the movement.

A sigh caught in my throat, my wolf fully aware of her current state. She wasn't in heat yet. Based on her scent, I'd give her maybe twelve hours before she was out of her mind with need.

But it would still be an uncomfortable climb to that state.

And then pure agony while she suffered through it without being knotted.

I didn't want to react. I really just wanted to keep walking. Alas, my beast forced a purr into my chest, one meant to soothe the shaking Omega in my arms.

She didn't immediately still, but her breathing noticeably changed.

I stood absolutely still, afraid that she might suddenly jolt again.

However, all she did was snuggle into my chest, like she was trying to burrow into the source of the rumbling.

With a sigh, I increased the intensity and allowed it to comfort her.

Which caused her to snuggle even closer. "Thank you," she whispered.

Rather than reply, I started walking again.

It wasn't until we reached the cabins that she said, "I've never had an Alpha purr for me before." They were soft words that sounded almost groggy. "I've never been knotted, either."

The confessions didn't surprise me. Claiming typically came with a knotting, which explained a lot about her hesitation where Alphas were concerned.

But I'd meant what I'd said about control—there were Alphas who could control their rutting instincts. And I was one of them.

Her *insults* had certainly helped because while my body was ready to go, my mind was saying, *Absolutely fucking not.*

She continued to nuzzle me as I walked up to the cabin I'd identified earlier as having the most supplies inside. It also had a heavy exterior door that would be useful for blocking out intruders. The glassless windows would be a problem, but I'd work on fixing that.

Just like I'd go play with the generator out back to see if I could do something about the utilities. From what I'd seen, there appeared to be solar energy panels involved. Which meant it might actually have some energy in it.

I used my boot to nudge open the door, my ears attuned to everything around us once more. But it was just as silent as before, my nose only picking up Riley's sweet scent and nothing else.

A full sweep of the area would be needed again soon because there was a good chance the Omega perfume was clouding out any and all potential threats.

The faster I moved away from her, the better.

So I carried her into the house and up the stairs into one of the two bedrooms and set her on the bed.

"There isn't any running water, but there's a well pump out back near the generator. I'll go see what I can do. If you want clothes, there are several options in the closet. And there's some canned food downstairs." I didn't elaborate beyond that, just turned to leave.

"Jonas…"

I paused at the threshold but didn't look back at her. "Yes?"

"I really don't dislike you," she said, repeating her words from earlier. "I'm sorry for always being rude. And for disrespecting you."

My jaw ticked as I tried to think of what to say to that.

While I appreciated the apology, I wasn't sure I accepted it.

For all I knew, she was just trying to see if she could persuade me to lose control and knot her, only to use it against me later.

It seemed like something she might do.

So rather than reply, I gave a curt nod.

And left.

I had a den to secure and an Omega to protect. That

was what mattered most right now. And I couldn't accomplish either of those things by standing in that room talking things through.

She could take care of herself for a bit.

While I took care of everything else.

SOMEWHERE IN NORTH CAROLINA

I paced the kitchen, frustrated.

It had nothing to do with the food offerings—I'd anticipated minimal supplies—and everything to do with Jonas's continued absence.

He'd left me *hours* ago. It was fully dark now. I could only see because of my wolf sight. But those same senses came with enhanced smelling and hearing, and I could neither smell nor hear Jonas.

He'd disappeared.

When I'd walked outside thirty minutes ago, I'd only been able to pick up a slight hint of his scent, suggesting he'd ventured off a while ago.

To where? What is he doing? Is he punishing me? Or is this his version of control—by escaping the Omega in heat?

His fury had been palpable. I knew I'd crossed a line, but I hadn't realized just how mad he was until I'd been right up against him.

Yet he'd purred for me.

Even while furious, he'd taken care of me.

Because he's always taking care of me. Even before he knew I was an Omega, he'd been there, guarding me and seeing to my needs.

It was his job to do so. But he'd taken it to another level. He'd treated me like I was *his*.

Which was part of the reason I'd been so hostile toward him. I didn't want to be owned or claimed or cared for by an Alpha.

I wanted my freedom.

And Jonas had just given it to me on a silver platter.

"I'm not going to knot you, Omega."

I'd thought he was joking. What Alpha could resist an Omega in heat?

But the way he'd flinched when I'd tried to touch him —something I'd done more subconsciously than consciously—had spoken volumes about his seriousness.

He really didn't want to knot me.

His body had definitely been ready before, and he'd even said he'd been about to knot me, but everything had changed the moment he'd left me on the water's edge.

Because up until that point, he'd thought my wolf had wanted his.

Which was when he'd intended to knot me.

But I'd reacted as a result of my wolf desiring his. I'd hated how weak that had made me. And I'd lashed out in the worst way—by bruising his Alpha ego.

However, this anger seemed to go so much deeper.

He'd claimed I'd rejected him. I'd corrected the notion, but it hadn't helped.

Because the truth was, I really had rejected him. For months. I'd been a complete bitch to him because I hadn't appreciated how I'd truly felt about him.

I hadn't wanted a relationship of any kind with the Alpha who'd provoked my inner Omega.

And as a result, I'd been rude, cruel, and downright *mean.*

So yeah. I'd rejected him.

Repeatedly.

All to run away from the truth of actually wanting him.

"Good job, Riley," I told myself.

As a positive to the situation, I didn't have to worry about him claiming me.

However, now I sort of wanted him to claim me. Because he really was a worthy mate.

He'd proved to be unlike any other Alpha I'd ever met. And I'd chased him away based on my past, all the while ignoring the present and future standing right before me.

I placed my forearms on the kitchen counter and bent to press my forehead to the marble surface. It wasn't chilled. It was warm. Just like the whole damn cabin.

I'd chosen a flimsy summer dress because of the heat. Nothing else. It had thin straps and a low-cut neckline and ended mid-thigh.

I was pretty sure it'd been meant for a child.

But I was five foot two and required smaller clothing because of my *Omega* sizing.

A low growl rumbled inside me, my irritation over everything coming back to the forefront of my mind. I'd been so rude to Jonas for something that wasn't his fault. Something neither of us could change. Something I'd been afraid of my entire life.

"You don't know a damn thing about me, Dr. Campbell. And you've never tried to know me."

Jonas had been right.

Yet also wrong.

I didn't know a lot about him, but I knew enough. He was a man of few words, existing mostly in his actions.

And all those actions had proved him to be a good Alpha.

Not once had he made me bow to him. Nor had he ever put me in my place, despite the numerous occasions where he should have done so. He'd always been cordial and downright *patient.*

"One of these days, he's going to bend you over and fuck that disobedience right out of you," Kieran had once joked after I'd not so politely excused Jonas from the room. "And you're going to love every minute of it."

I'd scoffed at the notion. "We both know that's never going to happen."

"On the contrary, *macushla.*" Kieran had bent his head to my ear, adding, "*You* are the only one who thinks that'll never happen. But someday he's going to figure out what you're hiding. Just wait."

"Well, he knows now," I replied. Not that Kieran could hear me.

I sort of wished he could, though. He'd have a solution to this mess.

Although, his solution would be to let Jonas knot me.

Fuck, he'd probably even advocate to allow Jonas to claim me.

"He grew up in Blood Sector," Kieran had said once. "I don't know him well, but Lorcan does. The two of them seem to enjoy being silent together."

I'd met Lorcan a few times in passing. He was one of Kieran's Elite guards. And terrifying as fuck.

Not unlike Jonas, really.

Because Jonas also had that brooding scariness quality to him. However, unlike Lorcan, Jonas had tried to be more approachable in my presence. He'd often attempted to engage me in polite conversation.

And I'd *rejected* him each time.

"Because I'm a terrible person," I told myself. "*Ugh.*"

I deserved this punishment.

I deserved to be abandoned. Alone. Forced to go through my estrus without an Alpha's touch.

It wouldn't be the first time.

Nor would it be the last.

I'd chosen this life of solitude. I had never wanted a nest or a child or a mate.

Because the right Alpha has never piqued my interest.

Until Jonas.

Which was why I'd pushed him away. He scared me. He made me question things. He caused my wolf to pace anxiously inside me. She wanted him. Even now, she was urging me to shift and go hunt for him. Because she wanted to be claimed. She wanted his purr. His touch. His *knot.*

How much of this craving is a result of the heat? I wondered. *Or is this really me?*

I could admit that I'd been attracted to Jonas from the first day we'd met. It was hard to ignore his beautiful face and thick blond hair and muscular form.

He was the epitome of Alpha male.

A specimen meant to be worshipped by my hands and tongue.

But this attraction went deeper than lust. It'd hit my very soul.

I'd just never understood how or why it was possible. Because X-Clan wolves didn't have fated-mate magic. We chose our partners.

And I'd chosen not to take an Alpha.

Hell, I'd suppressed the very instinct with drugs.

Yet that hadn't stopped my wolf from sitting up and taking notice.

I'd thought it was simply because Jonas was an X-Clan Alpha. But I'd never wanted a male like I did Jonas.

I'd found plenty of Alphas beautiful.

But Jonas took that to a whole new level.

His steadfast control, unerring calmness, and inexplicable patience all made him that much more desirable.

Just like his show of restraint tonight.

His confidence in his ability to harness his rutting instincts.

The way he'd carried me and purred for me even while being furious with me.

He was what an Alpha should be—*honorable.*

I should go look for him and apologize, I decided, standing upright.

I'd eaten a little after he'd left—just some random canned foods and old crackers. But it was enough to give me a bit of energy.

Except my insides were still rioting. I kept experiencing spasms that left me pretty much helpless for longer periods than I'd like.

I hadn't experienced one in about thirty minutes.

Which meant another pang was imminent.

I didn't want to undergo that pain outside while alone and in the wilderness. There might not have been any Infected close by, but all it took was one gust of wind going in the wrong direction to change that.

And then I'd become lunch to a horde of starving humans.

The disease had turned many of them mindless with hunger. Their bodies were deteriorating but not dying, the disease evolving to keep the host alive like an animated corpse.

It was disturbing.

And also part of the problem with our cure research—the humans were too far gone to be brought back.

It was cruel to force it after a certain point, and that point wasn't long after their initial infection.

My shoulders slumped as I took over one of the kitchen's dining chairs.

I'd spent so long searching for a solution, so long *hoping* for a way to save humanity, but it was becoming clearer every day that I'd failed.

Maybe that wasn't fair. But I felt like a failure anyway. And I despised that feeling.

Which made this situation with Jonas even worse because I'd failed with him, too.

"Pity party for one, please," I muttered at the table before me. It was small with just one other chair.

A chair that should have Jonas seated in it.

Actually, no.

Jonas should currently be fucking me in a bed upstairs. My wolf snorted inside me, obviously agreeing with the thought. But that snort quickly turned to annoyance—at me. Because *I* was the reason our desired mate had left.

I pressed my palm to my stomach, willing the next spasm to just hit me already so I could go find Jonas.

Naturally, it didn't come.

However, I knew that the second I left this cabin, my cramps would start again and send me to my knees.

So I'm stuck here for now.

I let my forehead fall to the table, much like I had the counter, and huffed in annoyance.

I can't just sit in this chair.

I at least needed to prepare. If Jonas really had left me

here to fend for myself, then I had to create a barricade. Or a proper den. Because in a few hours, I would be mindless with need and incapable of protecting myself.

But he said he would guard me, I thought. *Did something happen to him out there? Did he change his mind? Is he punishing me?*

I'd already considered that last question. Just like I'd wondered if maybe he'd run away to take control of his rutting instincts. However, he'd seemed perfectly in command of himself earlier.

So either something had happened to him—doubtful, given his skill set and expertise—or he'd decided to punish me.

Which meant he hadn't gone far. Just far enough for me not to be able to feel his presence.

So perhaps he'd set up a perimeter sweep, one that kept me safe while guaranteeing I went through this alone.

Asshole, I grumbled. But even as I considered the insult, I realized that he wasn't being an asshole at all. He was giving me what I'd wanted.

Which meant *I* was the one punishing myself.

How appropriate.

I stood again and started pacing.

I would need more linens. Water. And maybe a leash. Without restraints, I'd probably end up leaving the house to find Jonas. Or another Alpha.

Or anything that could fuck me.

This is why I hate being an Omega.

But rather than sit around and brood over it, I needed to prepare for it.

I was a renowned infectious disease physician.

I could handle a heat cycle.

I just needed to find the right supplies and barricade myself in a room.

I've got this.

CHAPTER 9
RILEY

I *soooo do not have this.*
I'm going to die.
Because I'm currently on fire.

I curled into a ball in the closet, shivering despite the heat surrounding me.

I'd chosen this small space for my nest because it'd made me feel safe. At least initially. But as the tremors had continued to rock my core, I'd begun to feel restless and claustrophobic.

A soft mewling sound slipped from my lips, my inner wolf begging for relief. Not necessarily sex, just *something*. Even an ice cube would do.

Because it was so damn hot in here.

Suffocating.

Lonely.

This was the path I'd chosen, though. The path I deserved.

A tear betrayed my inner sadness, making me want to

growl. *I am not this pathetic being. I'm Doctor Riley Campbell. I don't need an Alpha. I don't need anyone.*

Except that didn't stop me from craving company.

And not just any company, but Jonas.

I inhaled deeply, longing for his woodsy scent. His inherent protection. His domineering presence.

He'd been there for months, always staring at me, always guarding me. I'd taken him for granted. It seemed only fitting that he'd left me to fend for myself during my strongest moment of need.

Because I'd never respected him.

I'd never properly thanked him.

I'd never even been nice to him.

My knees touched my chest, the summer dress sticking to my skin. I whimpered again, the dampness between my legs sticky and *hot*.

So hot.

I swallowed, my throat parched. I hadn't been able to find much to drink. And as Jonas had warned, there wasn't any running water.

This is going to be a long week.

Fortunately, wolves were resilient. I could survive on little to no sustenance. It would weaken me severely, but as long as I survived, I should be able to make it to Fort Bragg.

Assuming Jonas doesn't leave me here to die, I thought sourly.

But no. That wasn't fair. He'd proved himself honorable. He might have been mad at me, but he wouldn't just abandon me to this fate.

This is just a punishment.

A way to put me in my place.

Because he's an Alpha and that's what Alphas do.

I hugged my knees as hard as I could, desperate to stop trembling. But all that did was make things worse.

"Riley?" Jonas's deep tones swirled around me, seeming to come from the night.

A lie.

A wish.

A fever dream.

"Riley?" the voice came again, making my wolf whimper a little for her desired mate.

It's not real, I told her. *It's our mind playing tricks on us.*

I'd experienced this before during a heat. Well, not exactly *this*. Because I hadn't known Jonas during my last full cycle. However, I understood how my brain crafted fantasies during these delirious moments.

I'd once let a Beta fuck me while imagining he was an Alpha. I'd fabricated a whole sensation in my mind of him having a knot, when he actually didn't.

It'd been excruciating.

And I hadn't let a Beta tend to me during my heat cycle since.

Because only an Alpha could truly satisfy an Omega during estrus.

Except now my chosen Alpha had a name. "*Jonas.*" Just saying it aloud had me clenching all over. And this was just the beginning of the hysteria.

I inhaled, his scent swathing me in a sea of momentary bliss that I knew would drown me in the next breath.

It's not real, I repeated to myself. *He left me. He abandoned me here. He's punishing me.*

A whisper of sound intruded on my solitude. My wolf perked up, my nose twitching as Jonas's scent washed over me once more.

God, that smells real.

I could almost hear him moving around the house.

His boots on the stairs.

My name from his lips.

His hand on the closet doorknob.

I closed my eyes, imagining what he would look like above me. *His icy blue irises glowing in the night. His hair falling around his face in feral-like waves. His stubbled jaw clenching. His hands reaching...*

"Riley." His voice had dropped to a whisper.

Fading.

Leaving.

Morphing into a—

His knuckles brushed my cheek.

And his purr...

Oh, wolves, his purr is the most amazing sound in existence. So warm and soothing. So perfect.

I leaned toward his touch, lost to this dream, lost to *him.*

The rumble increased, his fingers moving until his palm wrapped around the back of my neck, providing me with the dominance my inner wolf craved.

I sighed. "Jonas."

"I'm here."

"You're not," I whispered. "But that's okay. I understand."

"No, Riley. I'm right here." He put a little growl in his tone, chasing away a hint of the purr.

My brow furrowed, my eyes opening just a smidge. I expected the dream to end. But it didn't. Instead, his concerned face stole my vision. "Jonas."

"Yes." He gave my nape a squeeze and released me. "I had to find some supplies to get the generator and pump working. It's on now. We should have water soon."

He was squatting before me.

And looked like he was about to stand.

So I launched myself at him to keep him close, terrified

that he would leave me again. Fearful that he might *disappear*.

"You're real," I marveled, burying my nose in his neck. "Oh, moons, you're *real*." I couldn't stop shaking, my need to cling to him overriding all thought and reason.

This wasn't because of my heat.

Or maybe it was all because of my heat.

I didn't know.

I just knew that I needed *him*. Not his knot, but the man. "*Jonas*."

"Hey," he murmured, his arms coming around me. "It's okay, Doc. I'm here."

I shook my head. "You left."

"To gather supplies."

"To punish me," I said, not listening to him. "You left to punish me. And I deserved it. I've been... I've been rude. Disrespectful. I'm sorry. I... I was trying to push you away. I didn't want to *want* you. But my wolf. My wolf... I've had to take so many more suppressants to avoid *this*. To avoid *you*. I... I..." I wasn't sure what else to say.

There was so much I needed to apologize for.

I just wanted him to stay.

"Please stay," I whispered. "I know I don't deserve it or you. But... but I need you." It was a lot for me to admit. Yet not nearly enough. "I'm sorry for insulting you. For everything. I just wanted to irritate you like you irritate me."

I inhaled deeply, filling myself with his familiar scent. His strength. His *presence*.

Ours, my wolf seemed to hum. *This male is ours.*

I wish that were true, I thought at her. *But he's not ours.*

"I irritate you?" he asked softly.

"Not on purpose," I muttered against his neck. "You drive me crazy. Because my wolf wants you. More than she's ever wanted another wolf. That's why my suppressants are failing again already. I keep having to suppress her urges. And it... it made me so angry... at you."

"Because your wolf wants me."

"And me," I whispered. "I... I don't want to be owned. I don't want an Alpha to tell me what to do. I want to be free. But you... you made me consider other paths. I don't want to consider other paths, Jonas. I want my life. My *choice*."

"And you think mating an Alpha will change those choices?"

"I don't want a pup. At least not yet. But Alphas just trap Omegas in nests. They make them breed."

"Some do," he agreed, his hand rubbing up and down my back. "But not all Alphas do that, Riley."

I shook my head. "All the Alphas I know do."

"I don't," he replied. "I don't do that."

"You're not mated yet."

"By choice," he said, sounding frustrated. "You've never asked me about my past or why I make certain decisions. Like why I'm guarding you instead of taking over a clan."

I frowned. "Why do you guard me?"

"Because I prefer to be alone," he told me. "I like protecting others, as it's in my nature to do so, but I've never found a pack I wanted to join. Nor have I ever considered taking an Omega."

"But you said you were going to knot me."

"Because it's *you*, Riley."

"Because you realized that I'm an Omega," I translated.

"No." He curled his palm around my nape again, this time using his grip to pull me back and stare down at me.

"I've wanted you for months. Even when I thought you were a Beta."

"Why?"

He lifted a shoulder. "Your determination. Your intelligence. Your feisty little attitude. Your dedication to a cause. All of the above."

I stared at him.

"My wolf probably sensed your Omega designation," he continued. "But the man—*me*—has always wanted you regardless of your heritage."

"But an Alpha needs an Omega. It would have been temporary between us if I were a Beta."

"You make a lot of generalizations about Alphas," he murmured. "We're not all cut from the same cloth."

I narrowed my gaze. "I know there are different types of Alphas, Jonas."

"I'm not talking about *types*, Doctor. I'm talking about personalities and desires. Not all Alphas crave the same things in life. Maybe I don't want children yet, either. Have you even considered that?"

"No," I admitted. "But…"

"But?" he pressed.

"But I've never asked," I whispered. "I just…"

"Assumed?" he suggested, his expression softening a bit. "You've assumed a lot about me."

He started moving, making my arms tighten around his neck, my instincts forcing me to hold him to me.

"Please don't—"

He lifted me off the floor, cutting off my request. I was going to tell him not to leave me. However, this was okay with me. I immediately pressed my nose into his neck again, inhaling deeply and humming in satisfaction from his woodsy scent.

He purred in response, causing me to practically melt

against him. "I love that sound," I confided. "It makes me feel safe."

"You are safe," he promised. "I won't let anything happen to you, Doctor."

"*Riley*," I corrected him. "Please call me Riley."

"Riley," he echoed softly, his lips near my ear. "I made you a bath. It's from the well, but the cabin has a filter built in to help purify the water. That was one of the parts I had to fix outside."

"A bath?" I repeated.

"To help with the hot flashes. The water isn't cold, but it's cool." He carried me into the bathroom off the other room. I hadn't explored in here much. I'd been focused on finding a safe place to hide and had become distracted by my cramps and oncoming hysteria.

But his presence had calmed me again. *It's his purr. It's* him.

Jonas started to lower me to my feet. "You can—"

"Don't leave me," I interjected, hugging him to me with all the strength I had left. "Please don't leave me." He was helping me feel sane. Grounding me. Making me *human*.

"You need to drink some water, Riley. I left the bottles downstairs."

My throat screamed in agreement, but my arms clung to him. I'd never felt so needy in my life. And it had nothing to do with his knot and everything to do with *him*.

Jonas studied my face for another long moment. "All right." He readjusted his grip and held me to him as we left the bathroom to venture through the bed area toward the stairs. His purr reverberated around me as we descended. Then he bent to grab a bottle and handed it to me. "Drink this."

That was an order I wasn't going to reject.

I unscrewed the top and guzzled the contents, my insides sighing in instant relief.

When I finished, I found his lips curled a little in amusement.

"What?"

"It's just nice to see you obey a command for once," he said, taking the empty bottle from my hand and giving me another.

There were a lot of snarky things I could say to that, but I was too thirsty to comment. So I drank half the contents of the new bottle before focusing on words again. And all I could think to say was "Thank you."

"You're welcome." He bent to pick up another bottle of water. "Think you can hold a few more?"

I nodded.

He gave me four total, including the half-finished one, then started toward the stairs again.

"We have electricity now," he informed me. "But I'm keeping the lights off so we don't draw attention in the night. I also barricaded the doors and nailed some wood slats over the downstairs windows."

I frowned. "When?"

"Within the last hour."

"But you were gone."

"Before that, yeah. But I came back. I thought you were up here napping, not hiding in a closet."

"I... I needed somewhere safe."

"You are safe," he promised me as we reached the upstairs landing again. "I won't let anything happen to you, Riley." They were the same words he'd said just minutes ago, but they meant so much more now with my name attached to them.

I nuzzled into his neck. "I don't deserve your kindness."

His purr increased again. "You deserve far more than just kindness, Riley," he said softly. He took the water bottles from me when we entered the bathroom. "And now I'm going to show you what a real Alpha wants from his chosen Omega."

CHAPTER 10
RILEY

J onas set me on my feet and proceeded to kick off his
    shoes.

It was pretty clear to me what he had in mind.

And while I wanted to be annoyed, my wolf was
practically weeping with gratitude that he'd changed his
mind about knotting us.

I pulled my dress over my head, ready.

But he didn't immediately grab me. Instead, he turned
toward the cabinets and started pulling out soaps and other
items.

"Test the water," he told me.

Frowning, I turned and did what he'd requested. The
cool temperature immediately made me sigh, my body
begging me to dunk myself in the massive tub of refreshing
liquid. "This is a pretty nice bathroom for a cabin," I
commented distractedly.

"Yeah, definitely recently upgraded. The outside
doesn't look like much, but it's fairly advanced for a cabin

with all the energy-efficient tech." He turned, his zipper only partially done. "I already put some salts in the tub, but you may want more." He set the supplies on the edge.

My brow crinkled. *We're going to fuck in the tub?*

I almost voiced the question aloud, but the sound of his jeans whispering over his thighs had my gaze going right to his groin.

And that very impressive knot at the base.

Jonas caught my jaw and lifted my eyes to his. "Get in the tub, Omega."

I almost stumbled backward in my haste to comply, which elicited a low rumble of approval from him. But he caught my hip as I nearly fell into the tub.

"Easy, Riley." His amusement was palpable as he helped me enter the bath carefully.

However, he didn't just bend me over to fuck me like I'd anticipated—and *wanted*. He guided me down onto his lap instead.

Not facing him.

But away from him.

With my back to his chest and his arms around me, hugging me from behind. "Relax," he whispered into my ear. "I'll take care of you."

"By knotting me?" I asked hopefully.

He ran his hands up my sides. "By showing you what real Alphas want." His words were the same from before, but even more intimate now.

I shivered, liking the feel of his body against mine, his palms stroking along my skin, his breath against my ear.

"Omegas are rare," he continued. "They're meant to be cherished. Worshipped. *Loved.* Some say it's because of their ability to procreate and the sensations of exquisite sex. But it's about so much more than that, Riley."

His lips brushed my pulse, his teeth skimming the tender skin.

"It's about the soul bond. The connection. The rare link between an Alpha and his mate." He drew his mouth back up to nibble my ear. "I've never searched for this relationship because I never felt deserving of it."

I frowned. "Deserving?" I couldn't imagine an Alpha more *deserving* of a mate than Jonas. "Why don't you feel deserving of an Omega?"

"Because of my genetics." He shrugged, the movement causing his body to shift against mine. "My biological father raped my mother while in heat. He didn't try to control his rutting instinct. And I strive to be his opposite. Control matters, Riley. Control is the mark of a powerful Alpha."

"Your father wasn't powerful," I inferred.

"On the contrary, my sperm donor was very powerful. He just chose not to be a good Alpha."

"And you choose to be a good Alpha… by not taking a mate?"

"No. I choose to be a good Alpha by protecting those who need me. And I choose to be alone because I prefer it."

I understood that desire because I preferred to be alone, too. Just for very different reasons.

"The feeling that I don't deserve a mate plays a part, or it did when I was younger," he continued. "But it evolved into a sense of solitude that I enjoy." He kissed my pulse again, his hands moving to my stomach and downward to my thighs. "However, you make me want more. I've craved you for months."

"That's why I've always been rude to you. However, it wasn't because I could sense your desire." I'd known he was interested, but that wasn't what had driven my actions.

"It was because you made me want something that has always scared me."

My insides quaked as though to agree, my heat cycle making itself known once more.

I winced, my limbs locking from the onslaught of the shaking need destroying my core.

Jonas purred in response, his chest vibrating my back as he ran his hands up and down my sides again.

Never touching me sexually, just intimately.

Petting me.

Worshipping me, just as he'd said.

"Is it the thought of being claimed that scares you? Or the thought that being claimed will redefine who you are and take away your identity?" he asked softly.

"My identity," I breathed, my stomach churning from another painful spasm. "I like my freedom."

"I like freedom, too," he told me. "I like being able to travel. Live where I want to live and how I want to live. It's why I've not joined a pack. I think that makes us a bit similar."

"Yes." In a way, it did. "But you'll always have choices as an Alpha. Omegas lose their sense of choice when they take a mate."

"Only when they take one who doesn't value the Omega's free will." He kissed my temple, his palm going to my belly again. "I like you for who you are, Riley. Even your bratty side appeals to me. I wouldn't change anything about you."

"My bratty side appeals to you?" I almost looked back at him, but another cramp had me shifting forward instead.

His purr pulsed against my back, instantly soothing the ache once more.

"Your bratty side makes me want to fuck you," he told me. "It makes me want to punish you, too."

I stilled, my heart stuttering in my chest. "By leaving me to suffer my estrus alone?" I guessed.

"No. That's not punishment, Riley. That's cruelty." His palm slid lower, the tips of his fingers brushing the trimmed red hairs between my thighs.

I instantly shifted, wanting his hand lower, touching the needy space that wept for his knot.

But he kept his touch light, just grazing the top of my mound before gliding off to the side to trail down my thigh.

"Delayed gratification can be punishment," he informed me softly. "But only when done right. And not when an Omega is in pain from her heat."

He ran his fingers up the inside of my thigh until his thumb brushed my slick heat.

So light.

So promising.

Yet nowhere near enough.

"Spanking can be a fun punishment," he continued. "Although I prefer more creative concepts, like temperature play and feathers."

My thighs clenched.

"Prolonged gratification is another favorite," he added, his low voice unleashing a volcano of intense sensation inside me. "Making a woman come for minutes rather than seconds. Forcing her to beg me to stop so she can breathe."

He drew his touch through my sex, his finger unerringly locating my clit to give it a tender stroke.

"I think that would be an ideal punishment for you, Riley. Put that voice of yours to good use, hearing you *beg* me rather than *insult* me. Show you why my knot is the only knot you'll want, and prove to you that not just any Alpha cock will do."

"Oh God…" I was going to come apart from his words alone.

"Make you tell me a hundred times that it's my knot that makes you crazy, my knot that you've desired all along, *my knot* that you actually want inside you." He applied a little more pressure to my sensitive nub, his breath hot against my ear.

"Your knot," I whispered. "Only your knot."

"Yeah, just like that," he murmured. "My knot is the one you really *need*."

"Yes," I hissed, arching up into his hand. "I've wanted it for months. Since the day we met. And I hated you for it." *Hell, I might still hate him.*

But oh, I wanted him, too.

I *really* wanted him.

"Because you're scared of my claim."

"I'm scared you'll claim me," I echoed, slightly correcting his statement. "I don't want to be property."

"You wouldn't be my property, Riley. You would be my mate. My cherished partner in life. The woman I would do anything for, and the wolf I would vow to worship and protect until my last breath."

I shuddered, his words undoing something inside me that I'd ignored for far too many years.

"I don't want a nest full of pups, Riley. I want a happy mate who feels loved and safe, who enjoys being mine while ensuring that I'm very much hers in return. A partnership, not an ownership."

Yes, I thought, moving against his hand. *That's what I want, too. I want you.*

"Not all Alphas claim an Omega to own her," Jonas

murmured. "Some Alphas simply want a partner to worship for life. Just like I'm doing with you now."

He slid two fingers inside me and curled them in a way that brought instant relief to my core.

"I'm taking care of you because you need it." His words were a breath against my ear.

I jolted as his palm applied pressure to my clit while he fucked me fluidly with his fingers.

More, I thought, arching into him. *Please give me more.*

"I'm not owning you," he added softly. "I'm not taking advantage of you by knotting you. I'm just making you feel good, even when part of me still wants to punish you for every insult you've thrown my way."

I swallowed, my body burning for him even while my heart panged in my chest. His tone and words confirmed I'd really hurt him, which had never been my intent.

"However, I'm not punishing you, Riley. I'm putting your needs first. Because *that* is what a good Alpha does."

He curled his fingers again with his final three words, driving his statement home by forcing my body into a climax that blanketed my vision in bright white lights.

His name left my mouth on a pant as I grabbed his wrist and forced his hand to remain between my thighs.

Not that he'd tried to remove it.

He'd simply continued to stroke me, drawing out my pleasure while his purr soothed me with the comforting rhythm.

"Mmm, I could get used to those sounds," he hummed. "And the way you're clamping down around me makes me want to sink into your slick cunt and knot you for days."

"Yes." I pressed against his hand and then back into his groin. "I want your knot. Only your knot. No other knot."

"Is that you speaking? Or your heat?" he asked against my ear, a hint of sensual teasing in his voice.

"It's me. It's both. It's… my wolf." I shuddered as his palm flexed, my body more than ready to go again. "I want you, Jonas. I've wanted you since the first day I saw you. My Icelandic knight. My Alpha. My protector. My…" *My future.*

Oh, I was lost to him. To us. To *this.*

Maybe it was the heat. Maybe it was my wolf taking control. Maybe it was the suppressants breaking my mind.

But I no longer wanted to fight this attraction. I no longer wanted to hate him, to avoid him, or to dismiss him.

I just wanted Jonas.

"Knot me," I begged. "Please."

"No." He nipped my earlobe, my heart sinking with that easy denial.

He wanted to prove his control to me. To show me how an Alpha controlled his rut.

Was it because of my behavior? My rudeness? Or because of what he'd told me about his biological father?

His hand left my slick heat to trail upward to my jaw.

A tear blurred my vision, my heart seeming to break at the realization that he'd meant every word about not knotting me.

He gripped my chin and pulled my head back to look at him over my shoulder.

His icy gaze captured mine.

"I want to kiss you first," he said. "Then I'll knot you." He pulled me closer, his lips only a hairsbreadth from mine. "And once I'm deep inside you, I'm going to claim you."

My heart stopped. "Jonas…"

He brushed his mouth against mine, silencing me. "My wolf has chosen you. He's going to claim you, Riley. Just like your wolf is going to claim mine."

My inner animal hummed as though agreeing with that assessment.

She'd chosen him from the first day we'd met.

I'd just been fighting the instinct while being utterly rude to Jonas.

But he didn't seem to mind now.

His light blue eyes were intense, holding me captive as he said, "And after I claim you, I'll spend the rest of my life showing you what it means to have a good Alpha mate."

CHAPTER 11
JONAS

SOMEWHERE IN NORTH CAROLINA

I didn't believe in mincing words or providing false promises. I gave Riley the truth. Because if I knotted her during this heat, I would also be claiming her.

It had nothing to do with control and everything to do with my wolf's overbearing need to make this woman ours.

I could tame my rut and refrain from knotting her. I could walk away right fucking now.

However, the moment I gave in to her need, I'd lose myself to my wolf. I could control him. I could tell him to stop. I could even force him not to claim her.

But I didn't want to.

If she desired my knot, she would be receiving all of me.

Because I refused to go halfway with her.

Not after everything she'd admitted. Not after our last year together. Not after feeling her fall apart beneath my hands.

I was done waiting on the sidelines and bowing as required.

On this one thing, I would demand submission.

But if she rejected me right now, if she told me no, I would respect her wishes. I would finish our bath, put her somewhere comfortable, and go guard her to the best of my ability.

However, I wouldn't knot her.

Because at that point, she wouldn't deserve it.

There was a lot I would do for this female, but I drew the line at this. It would hurt too much to only give her part of myself, not all of me.

Maybe that made me selfish.

Or an asshole.

Or the opposite of a good Alpha.

But it felt right to demand this, to make her see how good we could be together.

Her wolf already wanted me.

Now it was up to the woman to accept me.

She flinched, causing me to release her chin. My heart sank as she began to move away from me.

I'd probably pushed her too far. Given her anxiety over the claiming process and the notion of an Alpha taking away her identity. I couldn't blame her.

However, I'd shown her who I was for months. If she thought I would be domineering and force her to be a breeding slave, then there wasn't much else I could do to change her mind.

"You grew up near Alberta Sector, right?" I asked as she moved her lower half away from my groin.

"I was part of a Vancouver area clan, but they had strong ties to Alberta, yes." She gripped the sides of the tub and stood, giving me a nice view of her pert little ass.

My wolf growled inside, eager to mark her there.

Not with my hands, but with my *teeth*.

She slowly turned around, giving me an eyeful of wet Omega pussy. I didn't bother to hide my interest, my gaze on that sweet heaven I might never experience. When she didn't immediately leave the tub, I slowly drew my focus up her flat abdomen to her pretty tits, and all the way up to her elven chin, beyond those fuckable lips, to her alluring blue eyes.

"Do you know how the Alphas in Alberta Sector treat Omegas?" she asked.

"I do." I'd never been there, nor did I have any desire to visit. They tended to form packs around their Omega mates, meaning more than one Alpha claimed the Omega. Given how much Alphas liked to fuck, it was fairly evident how the Omegas were treated in that sector.

Surely not all the Alphas were bad.

But the fact that sharing was so prevalent in that sector suggested they didn't engage in soul-deep bonds.

Because most X-Clan Alphas refused to share.

We were too possessive to even consider the notion.

"Then perhaps you'll understand my concern over being claimed since I was promised to one of their Alpha triads," she said quietly.

My eyebrows rose. "Promised?"

She sat down again, surprising me as she straddled my thighs and placed her hands on my shoulders. "My Alpha father arranged it. That's why I left." She frowned. "Well. 'Why I ran' would be more accurate. He hadn't exactly approved of my decision to move into the human world and pursue my degrees."

"Because he was an Alpha who believed in controlling your identity," I guessed.

"Yes." She moved closer, her slick heat only an inch

from my aching cock. "But you're nothing like those Alphas."

"I'm not," I agreed.

"You've never told me what to do. At least... not without good reason."

"Sometimes you have to obey," I told her.

"But just so we're clear, I'm probably not going to obey often," she informed me, her voice breathy despite her obvious intention to set some ground rules.

"I would hope not." I wrapped my palm around the back of her neck to pull her even closer. "I meant what I said earlier about punishments. I intend to do all those things to you."

"While still allowing me to be me?" she asked, her mouth close to mine.

"I've never desired you to change, Riley." I stroked my thumb along her neck. "And I won't be desiring you to change now, either."

She nodded slowly, her tongue slipping out to dampen her lower lip.

"Well, there is one change you'll need to make," I said, thinking it through.

She stilled. "What is it?"

"Your suppressants. I don't want you to take them anymore. I want you to be able to be you. I want your wolf to be free."

"But—"

"This is one of those items I won't negotiate, Riley. You can't suppress your shifter side. It isn't healthy. Fuck, it could have gotten us killed today."

She pulled back a little. "No one is going to let an Omega be a doctor."

I snorted. "There are plenty of Alphas who wouldn't bat an eye at that chosen profession." My gaze narrowed.

"Alphas like Kieran, right?" He was a V-Clan wolf with mystical abilities for healing. Surely he'd picked up on her penchant for suppressants—something I hadn't even considered until right now.

And her reddening cheeks told me I was on the right track.

I pulled back even more. "Has he knotted you?" Because that might prove problematic. "Have you used him to help you through a heat cycle?"

She frowned at me. "I told you that I've never been knotted. And I also haven't gone through estrus in over a decade."

Right. Yeah, she'd mentioned that. But the notion of her being with Kieran short-circuited my ability to process thought. "Do you want him to knot you?"

Her frown deepened. "No. Of course not."

"Are you sure?"

"I was just about to tell you to claim me, idiot. Yeah, I'm fucking sure." Her nostrils flared. "But now I'm not sure again because obviously you—"

I pressed my lips to hers, silencing whatever insult she'd been about to say.

Because she'd voiced the words I'd wanted to hear. *"I was just about to tell you to claim me."* The *idiot* part didn't matter.

Nothing else did.

Because Riley had just said she wanted me.

That was all I needed to know.

She mumbled something against my lips, but that mumble turned to a groan as I slid my tongue into her mouth.

Her slender arms wrapped around me, her breasts pressing into my chest.

And then she gave me everything I desired.

Her tongue was soft and explorative, learning my tastes and mimicking my movements with each stroke. She was bold. Adventurous. *Perfect.*

I squeezed the back of her neck to demonstrate my appreciation of her acquiescence.

Then I pressed my opposite palm to her rump and urged her to come even closer.

She didn't falter, her slick cunt kissing my cock in warm welcome.

I purred in approval and deepened our kiss, wanting to devour her and claim her with my mouth alone.

How many months had I dreamed of doing this to her? How many months had I milked my own knot at thoughts of this beautiful woman accepting me in her bed for even just a night?

But now I wouldn't just have a night with her.

I'd have her for life.

Starting with this estrus and leading into an eternity of calling her *mine.*

She moved against me, eager to do more than kiss.

However, I'd spent too many months fantasizing about that mouth of hers to move on from the task yet. I nipped her lower lip, lightly reprimanding her for trying to top from the bottom, and mastered her with my tongue.

Each stroke resembled a letter, spelling out the words, *You are mine.* Over and over and over again.

She melted into me, submitting entirely to my wolf and reveling in my growing purr.

It was all for her. *Everything* was for her.

Just like all that slick was for me. My knot. My cock. *Mine.*

I gathered her in my arms and stood, tired of the water and needing something more appropriate for our joining.

Her arms wrapped around my neck, her legs crossing

at the ankles against my ass.

I'd found some towels when investigating the cabin earlier.

Rather than dry us off, I grabbed them on our way to the bed, then threw them on the sheets to help soak up the mess we were about to make.

Riley would probably want them for her nest.

Assuming she could even fall deep enough into her estrus to stir that instinct.

I gently laid her on the bed, my lips still touching hers.

She drew her nails down my back, her wolf having come out to play.

"Claiming me already," I mused, situating us both into a comfortable position with our lower halves intimately secured.

Riley growled.

Or rather, her animal growled.

So I allowed mine to growl back.

She arched up into me in response, her body strung tight beneath me. "Knot me."

"Not yet," I said, my lips going to her ear to nibble her lobe. "I'm going to taste you first."

"*Jonas.*"

"Patience, Omega. It's my job to worship you. And I'm going to do just that."

Her sweet perfume practically suffocated me in response, my intended mate clearly liking this plan. Her nipples displayed evidence of that approval as well, the taut peaks practically begging me for my tongue as I kissed a path directly to her beautiful breasts.

They were the perfect size, fitting in my hand and beading to sharp little points of need.

I kissed the dusky tip, then laved the other one, making Riley moan and writhe beneath me.

Her heat still hadn't taken her under.

But it was close.

I could practically taste it on my tongue.

Her pupils were blown wide, her nostrils flaring, her lips panting.

Soon, my wolf hummed. *Soon she will be mine.*

I didn't technically need to wait, but I wanted to. There was something beautiful about claiming an Omega during the heightened state of her arousal. Perhaps it appealed most because I knew it wouldn't hurt her.

Any other time, she'd feel my teeth sinking into her tender skin.

And the mere notion of harming her left me uneasy.

I never wanted to harm Riley. Nor would I ever allow anyone else to harm her.

Which served as a motivator to continue my path downward because I needed to ensure she was ready to receive my cock.

Omegas were built to take their Alpha's knot. But that didn't mean it wouldn't hurt. Since Riley had never been knotted before, I needed to ensure she would enjoy mine.

"Fuck, you're wet," I whispered as I reached the soft red curls between her thighs. "And you smell amazing."

I was going to drown myself in her slick.

Cover myself from head to toe and revel in the scent of her need. Ensure everyone in this goddamn world knew she'd claimed me as hers.

"Remember what I said about punishment?" I asked as I settled myself between her splayed thighs.

She lifted her head to look down at me. "You said no punishment."

"No, I said I wanted to make you experience every single one I had to offer," I corrected. "How about we start with seeing how long I can make you come?"

CHAPTER 12
RILEY

My body *burned*.

And Jonas's words… his touch… his mouth… "*Fuck.*"

"Yes. After I make you come," he said, his lips right against my clit. "Ready, Riley?"

I had no idea what he truly planned to do to me, but I wasn't about to say no. "Yes."

"Good girl," he praised, his breath stroking my intimate folds and sending a shiver down my spine. "Hold on to the headboard for me, sweetheart. I'm not ready for your wolf to claw me yet."

I wanted to say something witty in response, issue some sort of clever retort, but words no longer existed in my brain. All I could think was his name on repeat.

He was destroying me in the best way.

And he hadn't even truly started yet.

"Hurry," I whispered. "I want to remember this."

Because once the heat overwhelmed me, I'd forget. I'd be lost to the rut. Lost to *him*.

Hell, I already was lost to him. I'd agreed to let him claim me. It was a risk. A huge fucking risk.

But it felt right.

And my wolf… my wolf wanted—

My back bowed off the bed as his mouth sealed around my clit, his tongue doing something that had me seeing stars. "Oh my… *fuck.*" I couldn't articulate what I wanted to say. Couldn't remember what I'd been thinking about.

All that mattered was his mouth.

His hands.

His *tongue.*

I barely noticed his fingers inside me, not even aware of when he'd slid them into me. But when he curled them upward like he'd done in the tub, I felt every inch.

He had to have at least two fingers inside me. Maybe three.

And he was moving them in a way that stretched me.

Preparing me.

For his knot.

Oh, moons.

Yes.

Yes, I want that.

I was borderline delirious, the room seeming to move in spirals of black and white.

It was dark. Then light. Then dark again.

The tree cover hid the moonlight, painting the room in shadows. My wolf could see, but all I wanted to look at was Jonas.

And his glowing blue irises.

Always staring.

Only, he had a very different look in those beautiful eyes now. He appeared hungry. Possessive. *Dominant.*

He sucked my sensitive nub, demanding my full attention as he pulled me into a cloud of ecstasy that left me breathless and panting at the same time.

I couldn't tell if I was coming, or flying, or dying.

Some combination of all of the above.

There was just so much sensation.

My limbs were tense. My insides were molten and twisting and spiraling and *climaxing*.

"*Jonas.*"

It almost hurt.

I couldn't inhale.

I... I was drowning.

Only to be sucked back into the living again with another nibble. *Right on my clit.*

"What are you doing to me?" I asked, my voice a rasp of sound. *Have I been screaming?*

"Punishing you," he murmured against my sex. "And loving every fucking minute of it."

He followed that up with another nibble that had me seeing stars.

I... I hadn't felt like this... perhaps ever.

My heat was definitely spurring this on, making me so sensitive that just a flick against my clit had me tumbling into oblivion.

Over and over again.

Making me come repeatedly, I thought, vaguely recalling what he'd threatened to do.

Fuck, if this was his idea of punishment, I was going to act out every damn day.

His fingers twisted, drawing me into yet another orgasm. Or maybe just a continuation of the one from the beginning.

Ripping and rolling through me.

Tightening my abdomen.

Wringing every ounce of pleasure from my veins.

Only for my body to throw me right back into the vortex of spasms and pleasure and passion, allowing me to receive even more.

I used to hate this experience.

Used to loathe the way my body craved sensation.

But Jonas was showing me just how good it could be.

And he hadn't even knotted me yet.

Oh, wolves. Just thinking about his knot had my stomach cramping with *need.* I wanted him inside me. Fucking me. Taking me. Driving in and out and *claiming* me in every way.

"Please," I whispered, my hips lifting to meet his mouth. "Jonas, *please.*"

I needed his cock. I… I needed to feel him fall apart. I wanted to experience the sensation of joining intimately with an Alpha.

Not to breed.

Not to create a true nest.

Just… just to be with him. To *feel.*

The Betas I'd been with had never been able to properly pleasure me. It wasn't their fault. Just biology.

But Jonas could take me to new heights. Hell, he already *had.* And that had been with just his mouth and tongue.

I screamed as he nipped my clit again, sending me spiraling into another dark, rapturous state that stole my ability to process thought once again.

My lungs burned with the reminder to breathe.

But I couldn't.

The air I needed didn't exist here.

Jonas.

The world was dark.

Jonas.

The world needed *light*.

Jonas.

I clawed at the depths of my pleasure, trying to swim upward, to find the surface of this suffocating euphoria.

Jonas.

Everything was on fire. My veins. My belly. My hands. Legs. Breasts. *Core*.

I was being eaten alive by *heat*.

Something big settled over me, dwarfing me, making me feel small and trapped.

No.

Not trapped.

Protected.

Lips ghosted against mine.

A tongue.

Air.

Jonas pushed a breath into my mouth, forcing me to inhale.

It was all woodsy masculinity and hot excitement.

My Alpha.

I dug my nails into his shoulders, my wolf having sprung free in her need to claim.

Just as he drove inside me.

Harshly. Thoroughly. All the way to the hilt.

My lips parted on a soundless scream, my lungs requiring more air to fulfill the need to yelp or moan or shout or shriek.

But Jonas was there.

Breathing for me.

Renewing my spirit with life as he claimed me with his tongue and cock.

His brutal pace satisfied my inner beast, her growl one I felt echoing from deep within. I pushed my hips up to meet his, my legs having wrapped around his waist of their own accord.

"*More.*" The word came from my mouth, but it wasn't my thought. It was from my wolf. Or an urge I was translating for her. I didn't understand.

Jonas growled in response, his own beast seeming to have taken control.

Rutting.

This was him giving his wolf authority to *claim*.

And there was nothing I could do to fight him. Not that I wanted to. Because my wolf had already decided to give this male everything.

She encouraged me to expose my throat.

But Jonas merely wrapped his palm around my neck and used his thumb to draw my mouth back to his.

He wanted to kiss me. Fuck me. Own me from the inside out. *Then* he would bite me.

I could feel the intention in every thrust, every tender stroke of his tongue, and in the intense way he held my neck and hip.

I was his.

Utterly owned.

Yet not in the way I'd feared.

He wasn't hurting me. He wasn't *taking*. He was giving. Just like he'd said he would.

And he punctuated that point with each swivel of his hips, the motion brushing my clit and stirring aftershocks throughout my system that felt a lot like additional orgasms.

This male played my body with the skill of an Alpha destined to possess me.

I didn't even want to stop him.

"Claim me," I whispered against his mouth. "Claim me, Jonas."

"I am claiming you, Riley," he replied. "Every fucking inch of you."

He punched his hips against mine so hard that I yelped, and then he kissed me again, chasing away any thought of pain with the worshipping caress of his tongue.

I felt drugged.

Lost to his savagery and completely annihilated by the reverence in his kiss. By the possession of his hands.

"Jonas." I clung to his shoulders again, my hands having wandered along his back and down toward his firm ass. But I needed him to hold me. To see me through this next part.

Because I was both excited and terrified.

His knot was pulsing. I could *feel* it throbbing between my legs. Ready to explode. To sink into my channel and latch onto me.

I knew it would feel amazing.

I knew it would give me the most intense orgasm of my life.

But there were so many unknowns with it.

I could become pregnant. I could be forced into a nest. I could be claimed and owned and told what to do every day for the rest of my life.

"Shh," Jonas hushed me, his lips tender against mine. "I've got you, sweetheart. I always have you."

He wasn't purring, yet his words resembled a soothing stroke to my senses.

I fell into his voice, his statement, and allowed it to encase me in a world of protection and grace.

I stared up into his beautiful eyes and let him lead.

I *submitted*.

Pride shone brightly in his gaze as he brushed a kiss against my mouth. "You're perfect, Riley," he told me. "So perfect and so very much mine."

Pain exploded in my abdomen as his knot shot up into me, a scream lodging in my throat and silenced by his palm squeezing at just the right moment.

I shuddered, the shock of his sudden orgasm and the cruelness of his palm startling me from my aroused stupor and drawing instant tears to my eyes.

But then the world shifted.

His knot did something... *Latching. Securing. Making us one.*

Oh... I convulsed as a wave of pleasure overwhelmed every inch of me, shooting me into the heavens once more.

Oblivion.

Warmth.

Insanity.

Jonas purred his approval against my ear, his lips skimming my lobe on his way to my neck and down to my shoulder.

"Stay with me, Riley," he whispered. "Be mine."

"I'm yours," I replied, jolting as his teeth sank into my skin.

Claiming me.

While his knot is pulsating inside me.

Making us one.

Securing us for a lifetime.

Euphoria danced through my being, my wolf rejoicing at the declaration.

My heart raced.

My lips parted on a breath as Jonas released my throat.

And all that left my mouth was a contented sigh.

Followed by the word "*Again.*"

Because the pleasure of his knot was waning. However, my heat... my heat was here. Overwhelming me. Sending me spiraling into a sea of *need.*

"*More,*" I growled, pushing against him.

Jonas growled in response. "*Patience, Omega.*"

My wolf whimpered beneath his reprimand.

"I'm going to give you what you need," he said, his mouth still against my shoulder. "But you're going to be patient."

My inner animal didn't like that plan at all. She responded by digging my nails into his shoulders and scraping violently downward.

Jonas caught my wrists and pulled them over my head. "Bondage is fun." The words were silky and smooth and *dark*. "Perhaps we'll explore that next."

I snarled.

He snarled back.

Much scarier. Much bigger. Much more *Alpha*.

"We're going to work on your patience, little wolf," he said, obviously aware that it was my animal leading me now. "But I want your human back for a minute."

My wolf snorted at that.

So he growled, this time far more intensely than before.

I quivered in response, then gasped at the rippling sensation stirring inside my lower belly from his knot.

"Jonas," I breathed, trembling.

"There's my mate," he murmured, brushing a kiss against my mouth. "You're disassociating a bit from your wolf."

"I... I don't..."

"It's okay," he told me. "I can manage your errant animal. I just need to know that you're all right."

"I'm... I'm overwhelmed."

"I know." He nuzzled me, his purr increasing. "But I'm going to take care of you, okay?"

I swallowed, my chin dipping as though he'd compelled me to nod. Or maybe it was just my inherent faith in him to protect me.

Like he'd been doing for months.

"You're my mate." The words were a breath against my mouth. "Which means I'm going to worship you for as long as your heat lasts. Then I'm going to cherish you for the rest of our lives."

My chest warmed at the thought. I wasn't sure what that entailed right now. But I trusted him. I trusted *this*. "Okay," I whispered. "I know you won't hurt me."

"No, I'm going to make you come alive," he promised. "You'll be feeling my knot for weeks."

My thighs clenched around him, making him growl.

"Yeah, just like that, sweetheart," he murmured, his hips moving just enough to make me moan. "I'm not going to hold back. Because your wolf wants *more*."

"Yes." I arched into him, my wrists still caught beneath his. "She wants to fuck."

"Then I'll give her my beast." He nipped my lower lip. "Because I take my job as your mate very seriously."

"You make it sound like a hardship," I breathed, my laugh catching in my throat as he thrust a little more.

"It'll be a challenge," he replied. "But I like challenges, Riley." He pressed his lips to my temple before whispering, "And you're my favorite challenge of them all."

"I'm a challenge?"

"*My* challenge," he corrected, his mouth at my ear. "The biggest one I've ever faced. And it only seems appropriate that you'll challenge me again now."

A quivering sensation stirred across my skin, my stomach contracting with a fresh wave of need and slick.

The world slipped beneath a black curtain.

Stealing my sight.

Blanketing my ears.

And leaving me in a senseless oblivion.

Estrus, I realized. *It's here.*

CHAPTER 13
RILEY

SOMEWHERE IN NORTH CAROLINA

I blinked, the world disappearing and reappearing some time later.

With Jonas rutting inside me.

With his mouth whispering hot promises in my ear.

With his hands on my breasts, my hips, my face.

I kissed him.

Bit him.

And fell into a cloud of confusion once more.

Only for his growl to bring me back.

Again.

And again.

And again.

It was a cycle of sensation, warmth, and me losing consciousness. Or rather, losing the war with my wolf.

She needed this cycle. And leaving me out of the fun was part of the punishment for my actions.

Disassociation. Just like Jonas had said.

But bits and pieces were clear, such as Jonas's affection. His purr. His kisses. His sweet words.

I felt him rotate me to all fours, his cock sliding into me from behind.

His knot pulsing.

His lips on my neck, kissing his claiming mark.

Water being forced down my throat.

His *cum*.

I came alive to find him lodged deep in my mouth, my throat working as I swallowed him down while he growled.

He tasted so good. So perfect. Like my new favorite meal.

"Fuck, Riley. I love the way you're looking at me right now." He thrust so far inside me that I worried he might knot my throat.

But he didn't.

He just squeezed the base of his shaft and unleashed more of his cum into my mouth.

I swallowed eagerly.

And then he was inside me again.

From behind.

From the front.

It was all a blur, my estrus muddling my thoughts and leaving me unfocused.

But slowly the world started to make sense again.

After hours, days, maybe even a week, of being fucked senseless by Jonas.

There were vague recollections of him forcing me to eat. Of my animal snarling in refusal, and him finding ways to tame my inner wolf with a few well-timed growls.

It was like some dark fever dream.

One I felt slowly releasing me from its grip as I stared out the windows at the trees. Sunshine filtered through them. And air stroked my face.

I glanced up to find the ceiling fan on.

And Jonas nowhere in sight.

Frowning, I started to sit up, but I immediately fell back as a spasm rocketed up my spine. *Ow.* He hadn't been kidding about feeling his knot for weeks. The damn Alpha had bruised me from the inside out.

"Riley?" His voice preceded him as he entered with a tray.

I blinked at him.

And he smiled. "You're awake."

I attempted to stretch and winced. "Yeah," I rasped, my throat aching from the attempt to use it.

"Here." He handed me a bottle of water. "Drink that."

I didn't argue; I just obeyed. Which required me to move a little, but each swallow seemed to cool the ache inside me more and more.

Then he gave me a plate of fruit, causing my eyebrow to inch upward.

"There's a garden nearby. No one has harvested it in a while." He shrugged. "I sensed your heat was finally waning, so I ran over there this morning to pick some fruit from the plants. I also pulled a few peaches off the tree next to it."

I picked up one of the strawberries and groaned at the sweet flavor. "Oh, this is good," I said.

His lips quirked up, a memory clearly lurking in his gaze.

I didn't ask, because I suspected I'd said something like that about his cum.

He settled beside me and eventually helped me sit up so I could eat more easily. But he didn't say anything. He merely brushed his fingertips over my bruises, his gaze assessing. And when he reached the claiming mark on my shoulder, I flinched.

His mouth curled downward at the tell. However, he didn't speak. He let me finish eating instead, which I was grateful for because I was starving.

I finished two bottles of water before I started to feel somewhat okay again, but I still ached everywhere.

He took the empty plate and bottles from me, then set them on the nightstand.

Another moment of silence lapsed between us.

And finally he looked at me again. "Are you all right?"

I touched the bite mark. "I'm…" *Confused? Overwhelmed? Pained?* I couldn't really find the right word.

My reaction seemed to unnerve him a bit because his gaze shuttered in the next moment.

"You gave me permission, Riley. You told me to claim you."

I frowned. "Yeah, I remember."

"Yet you regret it now?" he pressed.

My eyes widened. "You think I regret it?"

"Don't you?"

"No," I answered immediately. "I'm just… processing." There. That was a good word to describe how I felt.

His jaw clenched. "I smell doubt."

"Any doubt you smell isn't a result of me questioning your claim. I'm struggling to remember everything… after that. Up until now." I reached for him, realizing that I'd inspired this sense of uncertainty in him because of my behavior over the last, well, year.

His eyes met mine, the fierceness in them taking my breath away. "I don't regret it."

"Good," I told him. "Because I don't regret it either."

"Good," he echoed.

I arched a brow.

He arched one back.

"Are you going to kiss me now, or do I need to beg?" I demanded.

He huffed a laugh and shook his head. "I think I want to hear you beg."

"Oh, fuck you."

"That's not a very good start, Riley," he chastised me, but there was a smile in his voice. "*Please fuck me* are the words you're looking for."

"Maybe I'll tell you never to fuck me again."

"Then I'll growl until you change your mind," he replied.

I narrowed my gaze. "That's cheating."

"That's *biology*, Doctor."

An indignant part of me sputtered. But the overpowering part of me giggled. Because that was a clever play on words.

And he wasn't wrong.

It *was* biology.

An Alpha's growl instantly prepared an Omega for sex.

However, this Alpha didn't need to growl to make me wet. I was already soaked for him.

Because I wanted him. I wanted his knot. I wanted his purr. I wanted Jonas.

"Please fuck me, Alpha," I said softly. "But be gentle. I'm sore."

His gaze immediately turned liquid, his expression softening as he reached for me. "Want me to kiss your bruises first?"

"Yes, please."

"I'll start with this one," he said, leaning in to brush his lips against my shoulder.

My skin tingled in response to his attentions and to what it meant to be kissed there.

He was claiming me again.

But in a gentle way.

"I'll kiss every inch of you," he said as he licked a path up to my ear. "Then I'll give you another bath to help with the aches and pains."

I assumed he meant another bath like the one we'd taken together... whenever that was.

But then I realized he meant another one today.

Because he'd clearly recently bathed me.

As I'd woken up clean, not covered in our fluids.

And in a bed, not a nest.

I pressed my palm to his chest and glanced around, confused.

"What is it?" he asked.

"I... I didn't nest."

"We didn't breed," he said. "You're not pregnant."

My brow furrowed. "But I went into heat."

"After a decade of taking suppressants," he murmured. "I'm going to assume that played into it. Or perhaps fate."

I looked at him. "You're not mad?"

"Of course I'm not mad." He palmed my cheek. "You still have a world to try to save, Riley. Pups can wait. Or we can choose not to have them at all."

I couldn't help it. I *gaped* at him. "You... you would really be okay with not having pups?" He'd sort of insinuated it before. But to hear him say it again now, *after* mating me, somehow made it more real.

"If you don't want pups, then I'm okay not having them, Riley. I meant what I said—I won't take away your choices."

"But you'll have to take something for my cycles, then..." There were drugs Alphas could use to make themselves infertile during an Omega's heat. Many of them took the pills later in life when they wanted a break from raising children. It was essentially a male form of birth control.

Jonas shrugged. "If that means you not taking suppressants, and us still experiencing your heat, I'm fine with that solution."

I sat there and just stared at him.

An ironic response, considering how often he used to stare at me.

But I couldn't believe this male was actually real.

And not just real, but *mine*.

"I think I might love you, Jonas."

His lips curled. "Well, that's good, Doctor Campbell. Because I think I might love you, too."

I threw my arms around him, tackling him to the bed. "You're going to knot me now."

"Again, I think you're missing the *please* part of that—"

I kissed him.

Because we were done talking.

At least for now.

I'd give him hell again soon.

Especially since that apparently led to punishing orgasms.

But for this moment, I chose to just be with him. To kiss him. To make love to him. To cherish him in the way he'd promised to cherish me.

To *exist*.

And embrace this new path.

With Jonas.

As my mate.

CHAPTER 14
JONAS

SOMEWHERE IN NORTH CAROLINA

Riley and I spent another two days in bed together.
It probably wasn't the smartest decision, but I needed her reenergized and healthy prior to our journey. Which meant slower fucking, more baths, and a lot of meals.

Fortunately, she loved fruit.

And she wasn't averse to vegetables, either.

I'd hunted for some meat in wolf form. She hadn't been thrilled by the deer I'd caught and brought home, but she'd eaten it anyway. Because she'd needed the protein.

The soft pink tint to her cheeks now told me it'd been the right decision.

We'd both woken up with the sun, the light sprinkling through the thin curtains.

"You feel up for a run today?" I asked, my knuckles brushing her neck.

She nodded slowly. "A run would be nice."

"For eight or nine hours?" I pressed.

132

She looked at me. "Toward Fort Bragg?"

"Toward Fort Bragg," I echoed.

Her mouth curved upward. "Okay."

"We'll have to find another place to den," I warned her. "It's going to be a few days of running."

"I know. You told me we were at least two hundred miles away." She yawned and stretched, causing the sheets to pull down and expose her pretty tits.

I leaned forward to take a nipple into my mouth.

Because I could.

And because I wanted to.

Riley threaded her fingers through my hair, holding me to her and encouraging me to *suck*.

My perfect Omega, I thought, crawling over her and settling between her splayed thighs. *My perfect mate.* I slipped through her slickness, moving slowly, not quickly, and luxuriating in the sensation of *her*.

"You're beautiful," I murmured, my lips against her neck. "And you feel..." I slid into her. "So damn good, Riley. So fucking good."

She lifted her hips to meet mine, her motions as lazy and as slow as my own.

"Kiss me, Alpha."

"As you wish, Omega."

I nipped her earlobe, then drew my nose across her cheek before taking her mouth with mine.

Her fingers were still in my hair, but her opposite hand went to my shoulder, her sharp nails biting into my skin.

Feisty, I mused, loving her little claws.

I didn't pick up the pace, though.

I kept it slow and thorough, slipping almost all the way out of her before gliding back into her. She clenched around me, her inner walls demanding that I knot her.

But I valued patience.

I wanted to prolong the experience.

Make her pant for it.

She was so fucking responsive, her tight little body built to accept my thrusts, my girth, my *cock*.

I'd never expected to take a mate.

And now I couldn't think of a life without her.

My Riley. My Omega. My female.

I kissed her with every ounce of emotion I could fathom, wanting her to understand the devotion and gratitude I felt as a result of our union.

I'd worried she would come out of her heat and deny me. Yet she hadn't. She'd accepted it without a backward glance. Her only concerns had been around understanding everything that had happened. I'd sensed doubt in her, but it hadn't been the doubt I'd feared.

And I'd been thanking her with my mouth, hands, and body ever since.

She wrapped her legs around me, her sweet cunt rocking against me in a sensual kiss of bliss. It was an invitation and a taunt bundled up in one. She wanted me to fuck her harder while daring me not to.

"Vixen," I murmured against her mouth.

She smiled. "Fuck me, Alpha."

"I am."

"Harder."

"No." I nipped at her lower lip and went even slower.

She growled.

Which provoked a growl of my own, one that had her shuddering against me. "Yeah, two can play at that game, Omega." Only my growl made her even wetter and needier.

"Not fair," she panted, arching into me again. "*Jonas*."

I trailed kisses to her ear. "Patience, *ástin mín*."

She shivered. "*Ástin mín*." She seemed to be tasting the

endearment, or perhaps echoing it to make sure she'd heard it correctly.

"My love," I whispered, translating it for her as I slid all the way to the hilt inside her.

"Icelandic?"

"Mmm," I hummed, confirming for her.

"I like it," she admitted with a moan. "*More.*"

"You're gorgeous," I told her in Icelandic. "And very much mine. Only mine. Because I refuse to share you, my love. My wolf chose yours. My knot belongs to you. Only you."

She contracted around me, her body shaking from my Icelandic words. She couldn't understand them, but she certainly heard the sensual undertones caressing each statement.

"You like when I speak to you in my native tongue?" I asked, still slowly fucking her.

"Yes," she hissed, her claws biting into me again. "Your voice reminds me of your purr."

I unleashed a growl of approval and grinned at the way her body shook in response. "Do you prefer that or my purr?"

"Both. All of it. *Everything.*" She raked her nails down my back, her opposite hand forming a fist in my hair. "*Please*, Jonas. Knot me. I... I *need*."

I pressed a kiss to her pulse point, loving the way it vibrated against my tongue, and returned my mouth to hers.

She whimpered a bit in protest.

But that whimper morphed into a moan as I gave her what she needed, my hips pumping against her in a way that ensured she felt every inch.

"Touch your clit," I told her. "Rub that swollen little nub and make yourself come all over my cock."

"Yes," she hissed, her nails dragging along my lower back as she drew her touch to my side and then between us.

Her body jolted in response to her own stroke, making me thrust faster and harder.

My name left her sweet lips, her thighs tightening around me.

This position was more intimate because it let me see the emotions playing out over her beautiful face.

All hot excitement and painful expectation.

"Make yourself come," I demanded again. "Then I'll keep you there with my knot."

Her teeth sank into my lower lip, drawing blood as she fell apart beneath me.

It hurt in the best way, driving me forward and forcing me to follow her into oblivion.

Because my Omega had just *marked* me. Not just with her claws, but also with her teeth.

"*Fuck*, Riley," I groaned, my head going to her neck and down to the small crescent scar forming on her shoulder. I didn't bite her again. I merely kissed the healing wound I'd made during my claiming and rode the waves of pleasure with her.

She clung to me while I blanketed her in my protection and heat, vowing to always be there, to always guard her, to always ensure she understood what it meant to be mine.

We might not have had the most ideal of beginnings, but we would grow from that and become so much more as a result.

She released a little noise of contentment that stirred my purr to life. Her resulting sigh told me it was exactly what she wanted, the sound soothing her as she continued to convulse around my cock.

The perfect pairing.

A match destined for so much more.

I kissed my mark again before drawing my lips back up to her ear. "We're going to take a shower. Then we're going to eat. After that, we'll run. And tonight, I'm knotting you up against a tree."

Or perhaps that would become a noon activity.

I wasn't sure I could go more than a few hours without being inside her.

My wolf confirmed that notion when my knot subsided, his instinct to start immediately rutting again riding me hard.

However, I forced myself to slip from Riley's slick heaven.

Then I carried her to the shower—which was working beautifully now that all the solar tech had been figured out.

I would actually miss this little haven.

But we needed to get to the base. The others were likely worried at this point; we should have arrived several days ago. However, Riley's heat had lasted a week. Then we'd spent our two extra days in bed.

I didn't regret it.

And from the way Riley leaned into me now, I knew she didn't either.

She gave me a sleepy smile as I washed her hair. "I'm starting to appreciate the whole bond thing right now."

"Yeah?" I drew my fingers through her hair, combing the conditioner into it.

"Yeah," she echoed, her palms finding my abdomen as she rubbed soap into my skin.

When she didn't stray from my torso, I said, "There's more to me than my abs, *ástin mín*."

"I know." Her touch slipped down to my half-hard cock. She gave it a stroke before sliding up to massage my knot.

"Keep doing that and I'm going to fuck you in the shower."

"You say that like it's a threat and not a promise," she murmured, squeezing my base.

"Maybe I'll fuck that disobedient ass of yours."

"Maybe I'll like that," she countered, arching an auburn brow in obvious challenge.

I backed her into the wall, my hands in her hair, and pressed my arousal to her soft belly. She was so much smaller than me. Which only seemed to make me harder for her.

"I need you to be able to run," I told her. "If I take that pert ass, you won't be able to sit, let alone walk." I leaned in to press my lips to her ear. "But if you're a good girl, I'll give it to you at the base and make you scream for all the others to hear."

She shivered. "Yes, please."

I bit down on her lobe. "Show me you mean it and soap up the rest of me."

Her hands immediately started back up my torso, but this time she ventured to the sides and around to my back. "Such a good little wolf," I murmured in Icelandic. "Keep doing that and I'll give you even more rewards."

She responded with a sigh, clearly having no idea what I'd said but liking the tone of it just the same.

I kissed her pulse and continued my ministrations with her hair.

Then I took the soap from her and carefully caressed every inch of her.

She washed my hair while I knelt to reach her legs, her hands easily working a lather into my long strands before I rinsed us both beneath the single sprayer.

By the time we finished, I was more than ready to fuck her again.

But I didn't.

Instead, I focused on feeding her.

We didn't bother with clothes, just ate naked in the kitchen and drank enough water to ensure we were hydrated appropriately to run in this heat.

Once we were done, she nodded. "I'm ready."

"Good." I kissed her temple and led the way outside. "Let's go."

CHAPTER 15
JONAS

SOMEWHERE IN NORTH CAROLINA

Four Days Later

"I'm going to miss this," I said, staring up into Riley's beautiful eyes. The trees danced overhead, the full leaves blocking some of the morning sun, but it still painted an angelic glow around my mate's stunning features.

Her lips were parted, her cheeks a pretty shade of just-fucked pink, and her body still hummed with the aftershocks of her pleasure.

She'd ridden me this morning, just as she had the last several mornings, after sleeping beside me in wolf form through the night.

As soon as the sun began to rise, we'd shift, fuck, and then scavenge for food before heading off on our continued journey.

And today would likely be our final leg.

We'd made good time, covering a lot of ground during

the day before finding safe places to rest beneath the forest cover.

There'd been a few cabins and houses along the way, but we'd opted to stay in nature and let our wolves roam.

Mostly because we seemed to fuck each time we transitioned into our human forms.

Not that I was complaining.

I'd meant what I'd said—I would miss waking up like this every morning. We wouldn't be able to do this at the base. At least, not like this, beneath the trees and surrounded by the quiet sounds of the forest.

It was calming.

Almost a utopia-like setting.

Except all around us was chaos and misery.

Reality, I thought. *A reality that we need to return to now.*

Because Riley still had a job to do, as did I.

She lived through her work, and I now lived through her. If she wanted to spend the next century searching for a cure, I'd stand by her side and help in whatever capacity she allowed.

And knot every fucking morning, I thought as she bent to brush her lips against mine.

She smiled against my mouth, her breasts pillowed against my chest. "I'm going to miss this, too. But we can go for runs and replicate these moments whenever you want."

"Yeah?" I kissed her softly. "Is that a promise?"

"For when you're a good Alpha," she replied.

My lips twitched. "And what happens when I'm a bad Alpha?"

"Hmm." Her hips moved against mine. "I won't ride you when you're bad."

"Oh?" I grabbed her hips and flipped her, placing me on top. "Maybe I'll just growl and take you this way, then,"

I suggested, my cock still hard despite having just come inside her. This woman made me insatiable.

"Only if you promise to go down on me first," she told me.

I arched a brow. "If I'm being bad, I may not feel inclined to pleasure you."

"Then I'll act like a brat to inspire your version of punishment," she returned, her sassy reply going straight to my heart and stirring a laugh from my chest.

I kissed her once more, loving the way she felt beneath me and against me. "Would you like to know a secret, Riley?" I asked softly.

"Yes," she whispered back.

I pressed my lips to her ear. "I'll always be inclined to pleasure you. *Especially* when I'm being bad." I nibbled her earlobe and drew kisses down to her shoulder. "Because you're mine. And I will always want to please you, *ástin mín*."

She threaded her fingers in my hair to bring my mouth back to hers. "Can I tell you a secret now?"

"Always," I exhaled against her lips.

"I don't think you know how to be a bad Alpha," she told me, her voice whisper-soft. "You're so much better than all the ones I've ever met. And I'm glad I can call you mine."

"Hmm, so you *can* say nice things to me," I teased, nuzzling her. "I guess you just needed a good knotting."

She giggled, the sound one I wanted to hear over and over again. "Your knot is certainly a benefit in this situation."

"Is it?" I asked, nearly ready to fuck her again. "Would you like more of that *ben*—"

The hairs along the back of my neck danced, warning me of the subtle change in energy around us.

Riley stilled, her eyes on me. She might not have sensed the alteration yet, but she could tell something was wrong by my reaction alone.

"Shift," I demanded as I moved off of her. "Right now."

She didn't fight me, instead engaging her change in the next blink and rolling onto all fours. I stood, my senses coming alive as my nostrils flared at the scent of approaching Alphas.

At least two.

Maybe three.

And the aggression pouring off of them confirmed they weren't here for a polite chat.

"We're a little over thirty miles from the base," I said, voice low. "I'm going to lead you in the direction you need to go. Then I want you to run as fast as you can, for as long as you can, and do not look back."

She released a little protective whine, one that had a growl blossoming in my chest.

"This is not up for debate, Riley. *You will run.*" I infused every ounce of Alpha strength into those three words, my wolf refusing to consider any alternative. She would obey. She would survive. And I would fight these assholes until the bitter end.

Their lust mingled with their aggression, the Alphas on the hunt for the Omega they'd likely scented from miles away.

They wouldn't care that she was mated.

They'd try to remove me from the equation and take her for themselves.

Because everything about their approaching scent revealed one very important fact—these Alphas were *feral*.

They wouldn't be kind. Nor would they listen to reason.

Dominance was the name of this game.

And I couldn't play my part with Riley by my side.

She bowed her head, acknowledging my command. But not before allowing me to hear another whine. This one was underlined in fear because her wolf had likely picked up on the feral scent heading toward us.

I pressed my palm to her nape and gave it a good squeeze. "You are mine, Riley Campbell. And I'm about to demonstrate what that really means. Now let's run."

Her darkened irises met mine, a sense of understanding seeming to settle between us.

And then I leapt away from her to land on all fours, my wolf instantly taking charge. He remained acutely aware of Riley's movements alongside us as we moved, her scent the primary indication that she stayed close.

She was quick on her paws, allowing me to set a challenging pace.

But it wouldn't be fast enough to outrun the Alphas on our trail. They were hunting us like prey, and they would intrinsically consider Riley a weakness.

My weakness.

I would die for her. And they would anticipate that. Which was why I needed her to run as quickly as possible and attempt to reach a safe distance before the fight began.

If they so much as touched her, I would lose my control.

I'd *shred*.

And I needed my strategic side fully engaged and focused to be able to fight appropriately.

Because feral Alphas were savage. They fought with their teeth, not their minds. I would use that to my advantage.

Assuming I could urge Riley to safety first.

Otherwise, I would be too focused on protecting her to protect myself.

Once we reached the country highway we'd been trailing yesterday, I slowed and looked at Riley. I'd told her last night that this road led to Fort Bragg. I gestured now with my nose so she knew which direction to go.

But she slowed with me.

I growled and pointed again. *Go.*

She blinked, then flinched at a howl sounding in the distance.

Now, Riley, I told her with another growl.

She nuzzled my snout.

I thought she might have been trying to say, *I'm not going anywhere.* However, just when I was about to snarl out a demand, she bolted forward.

And ran.

Her reddish-brown coat glimmered beneath the sun, her sleek form fast and graceful and so fucking beautiful that it hurt my heart to see her flee.

But the aggressive air grounded me in the moment, seizing hold of my attention.

These fuckers had chosen the wrong Alpha to challenge.

I backed up into the middle of the road, wanting a wide-open space for the battle to come.

My nose told me that at least one of the approaching beasts was an X-Clan Alpha. But the other smelled a bit different. Not V-Clan—those were rare and not as prone to feral leanings—but some type of wolf. Maybe a Viking Alpha?

Regardless, they both belonged in Exiled Sector.

I could smell the foulness of their malevolent tendencies. These two creatures were broken beyond repair.

It could be some influence from the virus, but it was doubtful. Some wolves were just predisposed to going mad. One of them might have lost his mate. Or perhaps he'd spent too many months or years in wolf form.

There were several possibilities.

However, I didn't have time to ponder it now because they were coming, and if they defeated me, they would go for Riley.

Static energy rolled along my fur, causing each hair to stand on end. *Come and get me,* I thought, my wolf growling low in malicious warning.

The first beast burst through the tree line, his jaws parted on a snarl as he locked eyes with me.

There's the X-Clan Alpha. Now, where's your buddy? I wondered, my hackles rising as I sniffed the air. *Not far. But not here.*

I narrowed my gaze. *What are you two up to?*

The big black wolf in front of me didn't give me any answers. He just lunged toward me with a ferocious growl.

I dodged him, wanting to test his pacing on his feet, see what sort of skill I was working with here. He tried to rush me again, proving his lack of finesse.

But he was big.

And he definitely had a lot of muscle on him.

He pounced once more, his growl vibrating the air between us.

I spun away, then ducked and slashed out with my paw in time to catch him right across the throat.

His movements were predictable, making him easy to disarm.

Except he was feral, so a scratch to the throat—which was making him choke on blood—wasn't enough to truly take him down.

It only slowed his movements as he sputtered, his shifter genetics working to heal him as quickly as possible.

He kept trying to take me down, his reliance on his weight and size evident in each leap forward.

I hit him two more times with my paws, then did a jump of my own onto his back.

I caught his neck in my jaws and yanked to the side, spilling more blood.

His snarls morphed into gurgles as I kept gnawing at him.

Until finally he was down, soaked in his own blood, dying on the pavement.

It wasn't until he took his final breath that I realized his buddy hadn't appeared yet.

And his scent was no longer on the wind. At least not in a way that suggested he was approaching.

I spun around, searching for the trace of his aggression.

It wasn't like a feral Alpha to run from a fight.

Unless he'd caught something more interesting to pursue.

Something like an Omega.

I took off in Riley's direction, chasing not just her sweet scent but also the stench of aggression in her wake.

The feral Alpha had used his friend as a distraction, thus suggesting he might not have been relying solely on his instincts, but relying on his mind, too.

Maybe he isn't really feral.

Maybe he just used the other Alpha as a decoy.

Which means the real challenge is pursuing Riley.

Fuck.

CHAPTER 16
RILEY

The sharp aroma of aggression didn't fade; it *grew*.

I ran faster, hoping it was just the wind or the scent lingering beneath my snout, but my wolf knew the truth.

One of them is chasing me.

And I couldn't scent Jonas at all.

Is he hurt? Did they somehow subdue him?

It seemed an impossible feat to take Jonas down, especially that quickly.

Did one of the Alphas choose to chase me instead of battling my mate?

That suggested he might not be as insane as he smelled. Most feral wolves relied on their animal instincts, which typically meant removing competitors before rutting a potential mate.

But this Alpha seemed to be strategically pursuing me.

Does Jonas know?

If he didn't, he would soon. But would he be fast enough to help me?

My jaw clenched. *Think, Riley.*

I wasn't a normal Omega. But my wolf would submit if forced to.

Although, mating Jonas might actually make me less susceptible to certain Alpha tricks—such as their growls.

But if caught, I could pretend to supplicate.

And use his victory to my advantage.

Alphas didn't anticipate much of a fight from Omegas —something that might just give me an edge in this battle. Assuming the beast wasn't as feral as he seemed, anyway.

Which his trajectory and strategy had suggested might be the case.

I can't keep up this pace, I thought, my legs beginning to ache. A five-mile-per-hour pace was standard, but I could sprint upward of thirty to thirty-five miles an hour.

However, I couldn't hold that speed for much longer. And the Alpha on my tail was gaining on me, his size and strength no match for my own.

Fuck. Fuck. Fuck.

Think, Riley, I told myself again. *There has to be something I can do to distract him long enough for Jonas to catch—*

A man appeared in my path several meters ahead, his presence sudden and entirely unexpected. *A third Alpha.*

And this one had a knife.

But no scent.

Dark hair. Pale skin. A wicked grin.

How did he…?

But there wasn't time to think, not with the other Alpha growling behind me.

Supplicate, I thought. *Supplicate and use my perceived weakness as an advantage.*

I lowered my head, pretending to cower, and slowed my pace.

Jonas is coming. Jonas is coming. Jonas is coming.

The chant rolled through my mind, my wolf sure of his incoming presence.

"*Shift,*" the Alpha before me demanded. "Or I will make you shift."

Very coherent words, I noted, sniffing the air subtly. I hadn't scented this Alpha at all, the one behind me clouding my senses.

But as they both cornered me now, I could tell they were much less feral, suggesting they might have been using the other shifter.

Clever, I admitted, even while shivering.

Some supernaturals had opted to take advantage of this new world. We no longer had to hide. Humans knew we existed and were too busy hiding from zombies to care about much else.

Which left the wolves and other paranormal beings to govern themselves.

And some of those beings did not take kindly to rules.

These two Alphas seemed to fall into that category.

I stopped about three meters away from the male with the knife and bowed my head lower.

Then I engaged my shift, just like he'd ordered me to. Because I had no doubt he would carry out his threat to force me with a growl, and while it might not work as effectively as Jonas's would, I didn't want to tempt him into trying.

Besides, this provided me with an opportunity.

I slowed my shift, not only to give Jonas more time to catch up but also to appear weak.

The Alphas didn't rush me, their eyes too busy studying my form as I revealed it.

Another item to use to my advantage, I thought. *Alphas are always taken by Omegas. Even the feral ones.*

After several excruciating seconds—which felt like minutes—I finally stood upright on two feet. But I didn't lift my head. Instead, I studied the clothed Alpha's shoes.

Boots, I thought. *And jeans. Does he have more weapons tucked away somewhere? Another blade? Something I can use?*

"Your pretty fur matches your hair," he mused. "How beautiful."

I nearly snorted. I actually preferred to dye my hair. But the Infection had made that a bit difficult to maintain, as I couldn't just pop into a hairdresser for a spa treatment.

"Come here," the Alpha continued. "You and I will get better acquainted while Henrick handles your Alpha."

My jaw threatened to clench at both the insinuation in his tone and the hint of triumph in his words.

Handle my Alpha, I repeated. *Right.*

But I wanted him to think this would be easy, to lull him into a false state of comfort.

I forced my feet to move toward the Alpha, his scent telling me he wasn't an X-Clan wolf.

He wasn't a V-Clan wolf, either.

Or a Viking Alpha.

What are you? I wondered, inhaling deeply. *Not an Ash Wolf.*

Actually, he didn't smell very wolfish at all.

But definitely not human.

The answer came to me as he reached for my throat, his palm easily encircling my neck as he yanked me into his chest.

Vampire, I realized, my breath stilling as his nose went to my pulse. No wonder I didn't scent him. *Fuck.*

"Mmm," he hummed, his fangs skimming my sensitive skin. "Fresh Omega blood."

The wolf at my back snarled.

"Yes, yes, I know. We'll share. You just need to handle her *mate.*" His grip tightened against my throat as his opposite hand went to my hip, his knife seeming to have disappeared.

Into a holder of some kind? Or did it disappear entirely?

"You're even better than the bounty described," he whispered, causing my brow to furrow.

Bounty?

"Shall we keep her for ourselves, Henrick? Or use her before we hand her over?"

The wolf behind me grunted just as Jonas released a warning howl in the distance.

He didn't bother disguising his approach, the male Alpha wanting everyone to know that they'd fucked with the wrong shifter.

The world spun as the vampire whirled me in his arms, pressing my back to his chest. His palm remained against my throat, his lips at my neck, as his opposite hand went to my belly.

Alpha vampires didn't typically take Omegas of other species—unless they were V-Clan Omegas. While my blood might sate him, he couldn't mate me.

Although I could technically take his knot—something all Alpha vampires possessed, in addition to fangs—I very much did not want to.

And the other male was a Viking Alpha—something that was obvious to me because of his stark white coat and abnormally large size.

His scent also gave him away.

But I didn't know why he was on this continent. His kind typically resided near Scandinavia.

"There's a lovely price on your head," the vampire murmured against my pulse. "But they require you to be alive. Someone clearly misses you. Which makes me wonder *who*, as it's clearly not your mate."

I'd like to know the answer to that as well, I thought, frowning. *Does the international council think I'm missing? Are they using a bounty hunting service to find me?*

I supposed we were several days behind schedule, and it wasn't like Jonas or I had phoned in an update.

But to hire bounty hunters?

That didn't seem very council-like. They'd send out more military types like Jonas before they put up a call to rogues.

Mostly because of the exact situation I found myself in now—the hunters couldn't be trusted to do the right thing.

Jonas sprinted forward, his eyes a darker blue in wolf form and taking in everything around him in a single sweep of his gaze.

"Ah, welcome to the party," the vampire purred, his palm moving south, his intention clear. "I was just acquainting myself with your mate. Seems only fair after you murdered our pet."

Pet? I repeated to myself. *Does he mean their feral friend who they'd obviously sent after Jonas as a diversion?*

Jonas paused midstride, a wave of fury rolling off him as he took in the male at my back.

Henrick growled and lunged at Jonas, exploiting my mate's sudden stillness.

But Jonas reacted in a heartbeat, his claws slashing out defensively and catching the other male on the shoulder.

The two began to brawl in a flurry of fur and claws and *teeth*.

I shivered, the aggression making my knees go weak.

"It'll be over soon, little wolf," the vampire promised me, his lips grazing my pulse. "*Very* soon."

Jonas snarled, lunging toward us, only to be yanked back by the other wolf's teeth in his flank.

Shit. This was why he'd told me to run. Jonas's beast couldn't concentrate with me in another Alpha's arms. He needed me to be free. He needed me unharmed. He needed to know I wasn't—

Something sharp touched my throat, the vampire's palm having manifested the blade. "Ah, ah, ah," he tutted. "None of that."

I didn't understand at first.

But then I realized Jonas had his jaws wrapped around the other wolf's throat.

There was blood trickling down his chin.

He was winning, I thought.

He'd been about to win, something the vampire had clearly detected, and now...

Now he's using me to further distract Jonas.

CHAPTER 17
RILEY

These beings were definitely *not* feral. Which I'd already ascertained, but this just proved how cunning and cruel they were.

I flinched as the dagger bit into my skin, the sting eliciting a startled yelp from my lips.

Jonas immediately released the other wolf and took a step back.

And then he was suddenly on his back, the other Alpha having wasted no time in pinning him with his claws and teeth.

No. No. No!

This was not happening.

Jonas struggled, but the vampire just cut me again, this time humming as he brought the blade to his mouth to lick it clean.

While his opposite hand clamped down on my sex.

He hadn't touched me there yet, only rested his hand

right below my belly button with the clear intention of doing more—just to provoke Jonas.

However, now the vampire was claiming me intimately.

He was licking my blood off his blade and touching me in a way only Jonas ever should.

And it was driving my mate's beast insane.

The sounds coming from him reminded me of the feral wolf, but he was pinned, wounded, and no longer in touch with his strategic senses.

"Jonas," I whispered.

I didn't mean for it to come out like a plea, but the vampire's lips caressed my neck right at the moment I'd spoken.

My mate released a howl of fury that had the male chuckling at my back.

"So defenseless," he mused, his tongue tracing my throat. "Such an Omega."

My eyes narrowed at that, some part of my brain reigniting after having shut down through the shock of the last few minutes.

Hell, it was more like *seconds*.

Everything was just happening so quickly, the scene one I hadn't been able to fully digest.

Until now.

Until the vampire had spoken those last three words.

I may be an Omega, I thought. *But I am so much more than that. I'm an Omega with* teeth.

The Alpha was so consumed by my blood and licking it from his blade that he didn't notice as I initiated my shift—starting with my jaws.

Just enough to call forth my much sharper canines.

And then I went for the sensitive tendon between his thumb and forefinger while kicking back with my heel right against his shin.

The knife fell to the ground as I severed the tendon link with my teeth, and the vampire stumbled back in shock—a shock that led to him falling from the backward kick to his leg.

I jumped forward and immediately finished my shift, the change overcoming me so much faster after spending nearly two weeks with my new mate.

Fucking.

Eating.

Drinking.

And *shifting*.

Our mating had empowered me in a way I'd never anticipated, bringing me that much closer to my wolf's soul and allowing me to function as one being with her teeth and claws at the helm.

Jonas kicked the other Alpha off of him, his paw immediately reaching for me as he pushed me behind him and squared off with the other two males.

His growl was the most menacing sound I'd ever heard. It promised murder. It vowed to *protect*.

He didn't give our attackers time to regroup; he simply pounced, going for the vampire this time instead of the wolf.

Considering vampires—*especially* Alphas—possessed unnatural speed and strength, I understood his choice. Alpha vampires were vicious creatures, immune to sunlight, and bloodthirsty. I'd only been able to gain the upper hand temporarily because of the Alpha's distraction, and now Jonas was exploiting that injury.

He sank his jaws into the vampire's chest, weakening him further.

Before tackling him to the ground to go to work on his neck.

The vampire fought back, his arms wrapping around

Jonas and squeezing as the Viking Alpha darted forward to sink his own fangs into Jonas again.

Then the three of them became a blur of terrifying growls.

I took several steps back, but the glint of the blade caught my eye.

I was no match for these Alphas in wolf form, at least in terms of my strength and teeth.

But would I be any better on two feet with a knife in my hand?

A snapping sound distracted me from my analysis.

One of the bodies hit the ground.

Viking Alpha, I thought, relieved.

Until the vampire and Jonas started whirling around even faster. Their sounds were guttural and *wrong*.

I'd never seen a vampire fight a wolf. It sometimes happened, but usually only V-Clan Alphas fought Alpha vampires. And typically when protecting an Omega mate.

Another ferocious sound came from the brawl, this one unidentifiable.

I jumped backward again as they continued to move, the two Alphas evenly matched.

Or maybe unevenly, I worried.

Jonas was a badass and had been raised by V-Clan wolves. But he didn't harbor their magic. He wasn't vampire-like either. He didn't drink blood. He didn't hibernate. He was all X-Clan shifter.

My shifter.

My mate.

I had to do something to help him.

I just... I didn't know what to do. I wasn't magical either.

But I know how to cut open a body, I thought, looking at the blade again. *I know how to be deadly with a scalpel. Why not a dagger?*

I crept forward, only for the spinning Alphas to cut me off and send me several feet backward.

A crunching sound thundered through the air, followed by Jonas howling in pain as the blur slowed.

"You were an admirable opponent," the vampire said as he dropped Jonas on the ground, his muscles bulging from beneath his T-shirt, his jeans straining over his legs. "But not admirable enough."

He lifted his boot, the angle of it heading toward Jonas's neck.

My wolf reacted without thought, lunging forward, my jaws aiming at the vampire's throat. He caught me and spun me until he had me on the ground, his stronger body on top of mine and growling with pure menace.

But my animal didn't bow. She snapped at him, wanting to rip his face off.

Which made him *chuckle*.

Fucking *chuckle*.

"My, but you are one feisty little Omega," he mused. "I'm going to enjoy breaking you."

"That would be most unfortunate," another voice said, the Irish lilt refreshingly familiar. *Kieran.* "I rather need her whole."

I tried to look at him, but the vampire phased above me, distorting my vision.

"Oh, come now," Kieran drawled as he sent the vampire into a nearby tree with a wave of his palm. "Surely you're not already leaving? I was hoping to have a chat."

He forced the male to the ground with another flick of his wrist, his presence demanding that the other male *kneel*.

Vampires were exceptionally powerful.

However, Kieran was V-Clan royalty—a future *king*.

He possessed ancient magic. Magic I could feel now lashing out across the field and *strangling* the vampire. There would be no fight between them.

Kieran had already won.

And the vampire knew it, too.

"See, I put up the bounty knowing that all you hunters would eagerly jump to the cause and find Dr. Campbell. All I had to do was track your movements and allow you all to lead me to her."

Well, that explains the bounty, I thought, shivering beneath the wave of Kieran's dominance. He wasn't holding back his energy signature, ensuring everyone around him—alive or dead—felt his authority.

"But I made my requirements very clear," he continued. "I wanted Dr. Campbell alive and *untouched*." He glanced down at me, his sharp cheekbones accentuated by the clenching of his square jaw. "She looks *touched* to me."

I almost snorted in reply, but a shaky exhale from Jonas seized my attention in the next second.

Shit.

I immediately shifted back into human form and ran to him. He was no longer conscious, his bones seeming to have fractured around his middle. *From the vampire squeezing him*, I realized.

And he was covered in gashes, the combination of injuries from claws and teeth.

"*Kieran.*" I couldn't help the sense of urgency in my voice. "He's dying."

"Indeed," Kieran agreed.

The vampire shrieked, but I didn't bother looking at him.

It seemed Kieran had decided to apply the statement to the other supernatural.

I wasn't going to protest.

Nor was I going to give him the respect of even watching him die.

My focus remained on Jonas. *My mate. My love.* I whispered his name, my hands seeming to move uselessly over him.

I didn't know what to fix first. I wasn't even sure that I could help him. He was... he was bleeding. And not healing.

Barely even breathing now.

Fuck. "Kieran!" I screamed this time, my palms continuing to helplessly flutter over Jonas. I was a doctor. I... I had medical knowledge. I had to *fix* this. But how? Where? Without tools, without... without... *Oh, moons...*

I looked around, searching for something that could help. *Herbs,* I thought. *Plant medicine. Maybe. Something. There has to be something!*

The V-Clan Alpha knelt beside me, his midnight gaze on Jonas before looking at me. He seemed to scan my face and body for injury, his expression purely clinical. "Are you all right?"

"No!" I shouted. "No, I'm not all right. Jonas is *dying*."

"Yes," he agreed calmly. "He is."

"I..." I wasn't sure what to say. "I have to save him. We need... I don't know. I don't know!" The hysteria in my chest spread through my veins, making me shake.

Calm down, I told myself. *Calm down and focus. This is what you do. You save lives. Save Jonas. Save Jonas!*

But my wolf was panicking inside me, causing my heart to thunder in my chest. Her terror suffocated my ability to think, my soul already weeping for the male I'd only just begun to... to *love.*

"I see your secret has been revealed," Kieran said, his gaze lowered to Jonas. "He wasted no time in claiming you."

"I... I went into heat." An obvious statement, one Kieran had clearly already assumed if he'd put a bounty on his *Omega* friend—something we would absolutely be discussing later.

"And he claimed you," Kieran summarized.

"I. Yes. But I don't think... I don't think he had a choice." Not just because of my heat, but because we wanted each other. He was mine. I was his. Our wolves had spoken for us. The man... the man had just done what his beast had required of him.

"We always have a choice, little one," Kieran replied, his palms lifting to hover over Jonas's dying form.

He'd begun to shift back into his human state, his body revealing all the horrible injuries he'd sustained.

Oh, Jonas. I shivered.

"Can... can you heal him?" I knew Kieran possessed healing abilities. That was why he'd become a doctor, or rather, why he'd agreed to help with the virus research. But I wasn't sure how deep those talents ran, if he could help Jonas now or not.

"I can, yes." The V-Clan Alpha looked at me, his expression holding a note of curiosity. "But if he dies, his claim dies with him. It may hurt you. However, I can heal that pain. If that's your wish. And you could go back into hiding as you once did as a Beta."

I gaped at him. "What?" How could he say that? *Because it's what I would have wanted two weeks ago.*

But now...

"Or I can heal him for you," Kieran continued, ignoring my reaction. "What would you prefer?"

"Just like that?" I asked, my voice a whisper. "If… if I wanted my freedom…?"

"I would give it to you. The bounty only went out to a select few. They would be easily handled."

Handled, I repeated to myself. *As in killed.*

"You would do that for me?"

"Yes." He gave me a small smile. "I consider you a friend, Riley. Of which, I do not have many."

I could believe that, given his history and title.

"So if I want him healed?" I hedged, hope blossoming inside me. *Kieran can heal Jonas. He can bring him back. He can make my mate* whole *again.*

"I'll heal him," he answered simply. "But you need to choose soon. Or the choice will be taken from—"

"Heal him," I interrupted, my heart skipping several beats. "*Please* heal him."

Kieran studied me for another moment, that small smile seeming to reach his dark eyes. "As you wish, little one."

CHAPTER 18
JONAS

UNIDENTIFIED AIRSPACE

F*ucking Kieran.* When I came to, I was going to punch *Prince Charming* right in the damn mouth.

He'd offered to let me die, something I'd heard yet hadn't heard at the same time. I'd been lost in a daze, my soul trying to heal while my body denied the request.

But I'd been somewhat aware, my spirit tied to Riley's being and latching onto her warmth. Her scent. Her *presence.*

"If he dies, his claim dies with him."

Riley had been startled. But when it'd come time to make a decision regarding my life, she hadn't hesitated to ask him to heal me.

However, the offer nagged at me.

Hell, *Kieran* nagged at me. His heroic bullshit and smooth-talking had Riley laughing while combing her fingers through my hair.

Kieran had told her that I needed to rest. He'd put me

in some sort of stasis. But I had no doubt that he knew I could hear every fucking word right now.

"A bounty," Riley said, her voice holding a touch of annoyance. "For an Omega."

"Hmm," Kieran hummed. "I had sensed your waning suppressants during our last week at the compound. Remember?"

"Yes." She sounded disgruntled. "But I shouldn't have needed another dose so quickly."

"You shouldn't have needed them to begin with," he countered. "And I warned you last year that your wolf would learn how to metabolize them."

"That's why I was working on a more efficient serum, something I could have perfected had you helped me."

"You know I don't condone the use of suppressants, Riley." The chastising note in his voice grated on my nerves. While I fully agreed with him, it wasn't his place to chastise *my* mate. "It's unnatural to hide your distinction, which is why your wolf fought it."

Riley sighed, her fingers stilling in my hair. "That's easy for you to say. You're an Alpha, Kieran. That's a very different *distinction*."

"True," he conceded. "And I understand why you desired to hide. X-Clan Alphas lack a certain amount of decorum and skill when it comes to wooing their Omegas."

If I could have, I would have snorted. *Asshole.*

"Yes." Riley's easy agreement had me growling inside. "But Jonas didn't just claim me. He… he showed me what good Alphas want from a mate."

"Oh?" Kieran sounded intrigued. "And what does a good Alpha want from a mate?"

Her fingers combed through my hair again, all the way to my shoulders before leaving my mane behind in favor of my naked chest. "A partner." She placed her palm over my heart. "A lifemate."

Silence fell for a long moment before Kieran said, "Jonas is a good Alpha. He'll do right by you."

You say that now, I thought at him. *After voicing the option of letting me die.*

"I know he will," Riley replied, her palm drifting over my torso and back up to my throat. "I'm not the kind of wolf to obey without cause."

Kieran chuckled. "You will absolutely give him hell. I wish I could be around to see it."

"Maybe you will be."

"No. He won't choose to stay in Blood Sector."

Is that where we're heading? I wondered. *Blood Sector?*

"Why not? His mom lives there. It's where he grew up. And you have the technology to create a new lab. It makes sense for us to live with you," Riley said, her arguments sound, and yet the notion of living there made me sick to my stomach.

Or *sicker*, anyway.

Whatever magic Kieran had used to heal me had left me queasy already.

The thought of returning to Blood Sector and staying there just worsened the sensation.

"Jonas won't be comfortable in Blood Sector," Kieran told her. "He needs to be in a pack where he can stand on equal footing, and he's never had that among the V-Clan wolves. That's why he left."

Among other reasons, I thought, slightly miffed that *Prince Charming* had discerned these details about me without ever having asked.

"He's an Alpha," Kieran continued. "He needs to feel in control. He can't have that in my sector. Not because of anything I'll do, or anything my wolves will do—it's just a natural progression. V-Clan wolves and X-Clan wolves may be able to mate, but we're very different animals."

That was a polite way of saying that X-Clan Alphas were inferior to V-Clan Alphas.

I couldn't fault his logic, as it was true to an extent. All species had their own strengths. But the V-Clan wolves were notoriously lethal and ranked higher on the predator index than most supernaturals.

Vampires were one of their primary adversaries.

Hence my gratitude toward Kieran for handling the Alpha vampire when I hadn't been able to.

Most males in my situation might have disliked him for proving stronger and more capable in the situation. But not me. I wasn't too proud to admit that he'd saved my ass.

It was the aftermath of that situation that had pissed me off.

And his subsequent offer to just let me die, coupled with his easy candor right now with Riley.

Mine, my wolf kept growling. *Riley is mine.*

She and Kieran were friends. I accepted that. But that didn't stop my possessive animal from wanting to snarl out his claim.

He didn't care that Kieran technically had a mate.

Well, a *betrothed* Omega, anyway.

V-Clan Alphas courted their Omegas in very different ways, with Kieran's methodology being one of the most unique I'd ever seen.

Regardless, he wasn't fully involved with his betrothed yet, making him a potential adversary. At least in the eyes of my inner wolf.

"So where would you recommend that we go?" Riley asked softly after a long beat of silence. She'd likely been evaluating Kieran's words and realizing how true they were. "The labs have all been destroyed. Where will we continue our research?"

Kieran sighed. "I admire your tenacity, Riley. I always have. But we both know there isn't a cure. Not even my magic can heal them."

Her touch stilled against my shoulder. "You're giving up."

"I'm not giving up. I'm accepting fate. The best we can hope for now is a way to stop the mutation." His voice held a low rumble to it, the sound more like a growl than a purr. "Rohan called while you were... otherwise indisposed."

"And?" she pressed.

"They have a new case in Denmark. A Viking Alpha. Seems he transitioned last night and is just as brain-dead as a bitten Ash Wolf."

Fuck, I thought. That meant the virus had spread to two breeds of wolves.

"He's taking samples," Kieran continued. "I'll have them in the lab to review. But at this point, our focus needs to shift to containing the mutation. Because even with a cure, what would it actually heal? Once the brain is destroyed, there's nothing left but a shell."

Riley's nails scraped across my skin as she curled her hand into a fist. Her ire was like a whip to my senses, but she didn't speak.

She merely simmered.

"You know I'm right, little one," Kieran said, his voice a soft murmur that had me snarling inside.

I hadn't appreciated him chastising her earlier.

And I certainly did not appreciate him consoling her now. Even if it was what she needed.

"There's a clinic being established in Andorra Sector," he went on. "An X-Clan Beta by the name of Ceres is organizing it. Do you know him?"

"We've met." Riley's soft voice broke my heart a little. She was obviously angry, but not at Kieran. He'd spoken the truth and she knew it. She just hated that he was right.

Something I very much understood.

I didn't care much for the Alpha, but he was the Prince of Blood Sector for a reason. He knew what he was doing.

Which was why I had begun to suspect that this whole conversation—and his ensuring that I could hear it—was for *my* benefit.

He wanted Riley to be happy.

And he was guiding her to a place where she could prosper.

As my mate.

Had I been able to move my body, I would have clenched my jaw.

"The Sector Alpha is new," Kieran murmured. "He's looking for someone with your skill set to lead the lab that Ceres is building."

Definitely leading Riley to something.

She must have shared my suspicion because she skeptically asked, "Why not just give it to Ceres?"

"From what I understand, he specializes in turning humans into shifters. Specifically, X-Clan shifters. As a result, he would likely be a viable partner in understanding the wolf genetics. However, he lacks epidemiology experience. The two of you could make history together."

Clever bastard, I thought, almost amused by his antics. He knew Riley wouldn't refuse this opportunity.

"Are you trying to get rid of me, Dr. O'Callaghan?" she asked, the teasing note in her voice making my inner animal grumble in annoyance.

"Oh, *macushla*, if I could keep you, I would. But it would be a crime on my part to hold you back from shining like the jewel you are."

I'm going to kill him, I decided. *I'm going to rip his smooth-talking tongue from his mouth and make him swallow it.*

"And Andorra Sector isn't just an opportunity for you," he continued, that silky voice of his making my blood boil. "It's an opportunity for your mate, too."

"But the Sector Alpha likely won't let an Omega run his lab," she argued. "I mean, I assume he's an X-Clan wolf, right? Andorra Sector is all X-Clan?"

"Yes," Kieran confirmed. "But Ander Cain isn't like the Alphas you grew up with. His father is the Norse Sector Alpha."

Alpha Ludvig, I translated. But I already knew that, as I'd recognized Ander's name, too.

I'd met Alpha Ludvig before. He was a good wolf. Well-respected, too.

"I'm not as familiar with the European sectors," Riley admitted. "But X-Clan Alphas don't typically allow Omegas outside of the nest."

"Is that what Jonas told you?" he asked, making me want to growl again.

No. I did not tell her that, you fucking prick. If he would just let me wake up, I could speak for myself.

"Jonas isn't a normal X-Clan Alpha. He grew up in Blood Sector."

"Which I'm sure added to his charm levels," Kieran agreed.

Yeah, I'll show you how charming I am when you let me out of this fucking coma.

"But there are Alphas who not only encourage Omegas to do more than nest; they expect it. And Alpha Ludvig is one of those Alphas. All the wolves in his sector hold jobs, even his Omega mate. I imagine his son has been raised with a similar expectation, which is why he's already expressed interest in speaking with you."

Riley's palm flattened against my chest. "Alpha Ander has expressed interest in speaking with me?"

"Yes. He heard about what happened to the CDC compound and sent a notice through the channels that he's in need of an epidemiologist with your skill set."

"Does he know I'm an Omega?"

"Not yet," Kieran replied. "Only a handful are aware of that detail because of the regional bounty I put up. But it won't deter Ander's interest in meeting you. I suspect Jonas will be of interest as well, given his military background. Ander needs strong Alphas to ally with him if he wants to keep his new sector in line. Otherwise, he'll risk dissent."

Ander was only twenty-five, maybe thirty, which marked him as extremely young for leadership. His genetics were right, especially as Alpha Ludvig's son, but there would be challenges based on his age alone. He would need a strong team to maintain his hierarchy.

"And you think Jonas will prefer that over Blood Sector," Riley said, not a question but a statement.

"Yes." Kieran paused for a beat. "But you can talk with him to decide. If you want to remain in Blood Sector, I'll make you a lab. You have options. Consider them thoroughly. And remember what you said to me about Jonas."

"I said a lot about Jonas."

"Yes, but there's one item in particular that you need to keep in mind, *macushla*."

"What's that?" she asked, taking the question right from my mind. Because I wanted to know, too.

"Remember that he wants a lifemate," he said softly. "A partner. So be his partner, Riley. Talk it through *together*, and make the decision that's best for both of you."

CHAPTER 19

RILEY

BLOOD SECTOR

I lay beside Jonas in the bed, waiting for him to wake up. Kieran had given us one of his guest suites to use while Jonas finished recovering, which he'd claimed would be complete soon. "He'll move in an hour or two," Kieran had said before leaving. "His body just needs to catch up with his mind."

"What do you mean?"

"I'm sure he'll explain," Kieran had replied with a hint of a smile. "Enjoy, *macushla.*"

Darling, I'd translated, aware of what that little endearment meant. Kieran had only used it because he knew I liked the way his Irish lilt played off the word. He'd claimed my smile had given me away from day one, and he'd vowed to call me *macushla* ever since.

The V-Clan Alpha was a flirt. But it was all just part of his charm. Another Omega owned his soul, one he'd only mentioned a few times in passing. From what I'd gathered, they were playing some sort of game of hide-and-seek. That game was what had initially brought him to the CDC —his Omega had been hiding in Atlanta.

Then all hell had broken loose.

And he'd shifted his focus to using his healing powers to help with the pandemic.

But as he'd said on the plane, the cure eluded us. It didn't seem to exist at all, even with all our access to supernatural essences and genetics.

Kieran had been right—even if we found a cure, how much of the human mind had to be left for it to work?

I sighed, my head against Jonas's shoulder while I continued to wait for him to wake up.

"I need a new path," I mumbled to myself. "I can't give up on the potential for a cure. But Kieran's right about needing to shift our focus to the mutations." He'd mentioned Rohan's news about the Viking Alpha, which proved that another dangerous mutation now existed.

We needed to stop the virus before it started impacting X-Clan wolves or V-Clan wolves or W-Clan wolves or anyone else.

Except maybe vampires, I thought. *Not particularly fond of those right now.*

Although, Kieran had mentioned being friends with one. So apparently they weren't all like the monster I'd met roughly twelve hours ago.

The one who had almost destroyed my Alpha.

I pressed a kiss to Jonas's chest, right over his heart. "Thank you for protecting me," I whispered. "And for claiming me."

"You're welcome," he replied, startling me.

My focus shot upward to his face. "Jonas?" I blinked. "You're awake!"

"I've been awake," he grumbled, his gaze sliding past me to the nightstand.

I immediately moved to grab the glass of water waiting there.

Blood Sector was up and running as though we weren't in the middle of a pandemic. They'd protected most of Iceland's population, giving all the humans sanctuary within their borders so long as certain rules were followed.

They also had a blood ration in place—something the V-Clan wolves considered to be a form of property taxes.

Jonas nearly finished the glass of water, his head only slightly off the pillow to allow him to swallow, before saying, "My mind never slept. I've heard everything for the last... I don't know how many hours."

"It's after midnight here," I told him. "But it's been just over twelve hours or so. And you heard everything? Even the stuff from the plane?"

"And before that when Kieran offered to let me die," Jonas muttered. "Yeah. I heard it all."

He sounded angry, but I wasn't sure why. "I told him to heal you. I didn't even hesitate. You know that, right?"

His expression softened a little. "I know, *ástin mín*."

"Then why are you angry?"

And there went the softness in his facial gestures, leaving behind a sharp jaw dotted with blond hairs. It'd been a while since he'd been able to shave. But I had to admit, I rather liked the thin beard he was growing.

"Oh, I don't know, *macushla*. It could be Kieran's belittling my life's worth, or his incessant flirtation, or his constant commentary on the intentions of X-Clan Alphas. You tell me."

I stared at him for a minute.

My lips started to twitch when I realized the true cause of his anger.

Yeah, part of it probably was related to Kieran's offer regarding my future path, but that wasn't the true heart of Jonas's ire. "You're jealous."

"Fuck yes, I'm jealous," he returned, surprising me with his vehemence. "You're *mine*. And he keeps flirting with *my* mate. My wolf wants to shred him."

My smile grew, which only made his eyes narrow. "You know he's just a friend, right?"

"A friend who wants to *keep* you," he returned, causing my eyebrows to lift. "Yeah, I heard that part, too."

"He meant as a physician and a friend."

"Sure he did."

I rolled my eyes. "He's already mated."

"He's betrothed," Jonas replied. "That's not the same as being mated. And his betrothed isn't even here."

"True," I agreed. "But he's only ever been a friend to me. And a very useful collaborator."

Jonas snorted.

"He saved your life," I pointed out. "You can't really hate him."

"I certainly don't have to *like* him either, though."

"Stubborn Alpha," I mused.

"Stubborn Omega," he returned without missing a beat.

"Then I guess we were made for each other," I said as I straddled his hips and pressed my palms to his chest to sit upward on top of him. "Want to knot me so everyone knows I'm yours?" I rubbed against him in invitation, which stirred a deep growl from his chest.

A growl that immediately had my insides reacting.

Slick pooled at my core, coating his already hard cock.

I'd stripped out of the clothes Kieran had lent me prior to lying with Jonas in the bed.

Definitely a brilliant decision on my part, I thought as I rocked against him.

He growled again, his hands going to my hips as he flipped us and entered me without warning.

I jolted against him, my hips flexing on instinct while I moaned. That had hurt in the *best* way.

"More," I begged as he stilled.

"Tell me my knot is the only one you need."

"Your knot is the only one I *want* and need," I promised him, my hands grasping his shoulders. "You're my mate, Jonas. By choice. And I will always need and want you."

He cupped my cheek, his icy gaze intense. "I love you, Riley."

"Prove it," I countered, lifting my hips again. "Knot me."

He chuckled. "Always so demanding."

"Yep." I wrapped my legs around him. "Now, Alpha."

He caught my lower lip between his teeth and nibbled. Not hard, just enough to warn. "You're a brat, Riley Campbell."

"Does that mean you're going to punish me?" I asked, hopeful.

He sighed. "I nearly die, and your response is to demand sex the moment I wake up."

"Yes." Because it proved he was alive. It helped me feel grounded again. Claimed. *Loved*. "I need your knot, Jonas," I told him again, meaning every word. "*Your* knot."

He moved against me, his nose brushing mine. "I'm proud of you for fighting," he whispered. "So damn proud to call you mine. Never lose that fire, Riley. It's who you are, who I *love*."

I shuddered beneath him, my heart beating a mile a

minute as I accepted his praise and allowed it to deepen our embrace. "You're who I love, too."

It was a truth my wolf had known from the beginning —this Alpha had always been our destiny.

But now I understood that future, too.

"I want to be where you are. Always." Something I'd realized while speaking with Kieran about where to go next.

He was right about Jonas needing a purpose.

And that purpose would be more pronounced in an X-Clan sector where he could be true to his Alpha roots.

He needed to feel superior, but not because of his arrogance or pride—it was just how he thrived.

Jonas kissed me, his lips and tongue whispering his affection and devotion with each stroke as he made love to me below.

It was slow.

Tender.

Perfection.

I didn't want fast or hard. I wanted this—a vow of life.

Jonas is healed. We're safe. We're meant to be together.

Yet another reason to leave Blood Sector—I didn't want to be near their vampire neighbors in Greenland. Sure, the ocean was large. But the relations between V-Clan wolves and the vampire species were a little too close for comfort.

Especially after my most recent experience.

Andorra Sector was safer. In theory, anyway.

Jonas nipped my lower lip, drawing me back to him as he slid in deep.

Still slow and purposeful.

Still beautifully *us.*

I sighed, my wolf pleased with her Alpha's attentions.

His hands roamed up my sides, his palms cupping my breasts before venturing up to capture my face.

He pulled away to stare down at me, his gaze glittering with possession as he moved in and out of me.

No words.

Just emotions.

Love. Passion. Promises of forever.

He maintained his stare as he drove me to oblivion, and continued to watch me as his knot claimed me from the inside.

So intense. And exactly what I craved.

He kissed me again as the waves of pleasure rocketed through both of us, his low growls a rumble against my chest.

A rumble that turned into a purr.

I melted beneath him, that sound easily my favorite addiction. "You're mine," he whispered.

"Yes," I agreed, my nails digging into his nape a little as I held him to me. "And you're mine."

He smiled against my mouth and kissed me soundly again.

And when his knot released me, he carried me across the guest suite to the adjoining bathroom.

Where he bathed me.

Purred for me.

And washed all the blood from his own skin. I'd tried to wipe him clean on the plane with the towels Kieran had provided. But running water definitely helped.

It wasn't until we were drying off that Jonas said, "If you asked me to stay here, I would. For you."

"I know." He'd more than proved to me that he would always put my desires first. But that wasn't what it meant to be lifemates, as Kieran had so helpfully pointed out.

The V-Clan Alpha was certainly an enigma, always

providing wise words while ensuring I could read between the lines at the same time.

He wasn't like that with others. Actually, he could come across as downright cold.

But never with me.

Not for romantic reasons, though.

We were friends. Just like I'd told Jonas. Two researchers at heart who both maintained a similar form of respect for humanity.

His was more cynical in nature. Mine was more hopeful. However, that was what helped us balance each other.

"I want to talk to the Andorra Sector Alpha," I told Jonas after a beat. "I want to hear more about his clinic. And maybe speak to Beta Ceres about his research, too."

"Are you sure?" Jonas asked.

I nodded. "It's what makes sense for *us*, Jonas. And Kieran was right about the potential collaboration there." I studied my mate as he wrapped a towel around his waist. "Are you interested in Andorra Sector?"

"I'm interested in discussing the option with Ander, yes," he said. "I'm familiar with his father, Ludvig. He's a good wolf. If Ander has turned into anything like him, which I imagine he has if he's already taking over a sector, then Andorra may be a good place for us."

"Because you could be an enforcer?" I wondered aloud.

"Because Ander will treat you as he should—as a world-renowned researcher with the potential to ensure that our species survives this pandemic."

Not an Omega or the cherished mate of an Alpha, but as a position of worth, I thought. "You think he'll be respectful of my dreams?"

"There's only one way to find out." Jonas stepped up to

179

me, his palm curling around my nape as he stared down into my eyes. "I won't ever put you in a position where you feel inferior. Nor will I allow anyone else to do so."

I smiled up at him. "I'm not sure I'll allow it either."

His lips quirked at the sides. "I'm counting on that, *ástin mín.*" He brushed his mouth against mine. "We'll see if Ander lives up to our expectations and go from there."

"Okay," I whispered.

"Okay," he echoed, kissing me again. "We're in this together, *ástin mín.* For always."

"For always," I repeated, smiling. "But don't think that means I plan to behave."

He snorted. "Sweetheart, I will never expect you to *behave.* I know better."

"Good." I nibbled his lower lip. "Want to knot me again?"

A laugh escaped him. "I'll always want to knot you, but I need some food first, Omega."

I feigned a pout. "But…"

He nipped at my lower lip and pressed his mouth to my ear. "Patience, Riley." The words came out in a growl. "I'll satisfy you once I've eaten. Now get dressed."

I heaved a long, dramatic sigh. "I'm going to have to insult your knot again, aren't I?"

"Try it and you'll regret it."

"Not with your version of punishment," I murmured.

He smacked my ass hard enough to make me yelp. "Stop torturing me, Omega. I need food."

I pretended to pout again but went in search of clothes.

All the while, he observed me with hungry eyes.

It was clear that while he might require a meal, I would definitely be dessert.

And I couldn't wait.

Mine, I thought. *This Alpha is all mine.*

EPILOGUE

JONAS

ANDORRA SECTOR

Ander Cain didn't smile. He merely stared, his severe presence reminding me of a much more stoic version of his father.

Perhaps it's his Omega that softens him, I thought, thinking of Ludvig. *Or the family he's created.*

Because Ander lacked his father's warmth.

But he wasn't cruel or particularly rude. He sat across from Riley and listened as she explained her research and credentials. Something told me he already knew everything she told him now. However, he didn't interrupt her. Nor did he make her bow or supplicate.

Which was a point in his favor.

Actually, he'd received *several* points.

He'd met us on the tarmac with his second-in-command—Elias, who sat beside him and therefore across from me at the table—and had led us into a building that had clearly been constructed recently.

Rather than immediately interrogate us, he'd shown us

the labs and introduced Riley to Ceres. The two of them had spoken a few times over the phone already, as Andorra Sector's technology capabilities were compatible with those of Blood Sector.

Although, Blood Sector was arguably more futuristic in nature. Which was par for the course, considering the mystical essence of the beings who lived there.

Still, Andorra Sector held a certain appeal that I couldn't deny. Not just because of the leadership, but because of the general aura and appearance.

I felt comfortable here.

And Riley's eager tones now told me she did, too.

Her excitement had started in the labs after meeting Ceres face-to-face. He'd shown her something he was working on, and she'd jumped into some highly scientific discussion with him that I hadn't understood.

Elias and Ander had shared a glance, suggesting that they hadn't understood it either.

But whatever it was had pleased my mate. Which had left me pleased as a result.

And now she was trying to sell herself for a position that Ander had clearly already decided to give her.

I could see it in his expression.

However, he remained quiet and listened, his golden irises swirling with knowledge.

Definitely his father's son, I decided. *Apart from the colder demeanor*. But I could work with that.

I didn't like chatting unnecessarily, so if he wanted to keep it to a minimum, by all means.

His second-in-command seemed a little less stoic. His midnight gaze matched his thick, dark hair—which he'd run his fingers through a few times while sitting here, suggesting he didn't like to remain still.

Elias had smiled at Riley a few times, mostly to

encourage her to continue speaking. It had seemed innocent enough—just the usual adoration that Alphas exuded around Omegas.

Although, Ander hadn't been adoring at all. He'd been all business with Riley, treating her as though she were another Alpha.

That was his father's influence.

And it was what made Riley almost instantly comfortable in his presence.

She stole a deep breath and concluded with, "So as a result, I think this would be a very good fit for me."

Ander waited a beat, his golden irises assessing her. "I agree."

Elias nodded.

"What are your requirements?" Ander asked her. "Lodging, obviously. But do you have a preference on rooms? Location? We have suites here in this building, but also cabins and other styles of homes throughout the sector."

Riley glanced at me.

I didn't have a preference. I would go wherever Riley desired.

"Is that something we can perhaps see on a tour and then decide?" she asked slowly, her focus returning to Ander.

"Absolutely," Ander agreed. "Elias can help arrange a proper tour of options. In the interim, you can stay in a guest suite here."

"You may want two locations," Elias added. "We have a lot of Alphas in this sector. There are certain times where that may prove problematic."

"How problematic?" I asked, my gaze narrowing. Because I knew *exactly* what that meant.

"I'm not going to sugarcoat it. There are Alphas here

who don't believe I'm old enough to lead. Challenges are frequent. I've yet to lose one." That last part seemed like a bit of a warning.

He would be able to sense my dominance as a fellow Alpha. I wasn't just older than him, but perhaps even stronger. Which made me a clear threat to his leadership.

Except I had no desire to take his job.

"I don't envy you your position," I informed him. "But I'll help you protect it so long as a few of my terms are met."

Riley glanced at me in surprise. We hadn't discussed this part of the conversation, mostly because I hadn't been sure this would be necessary. I'd wanted to observe her reactions first. Now that I knew she wanted to stay, I could list my demands.

"Name them," Ander said, his expression unchanged. But Elias appeared intrigued beside him, while also seeming a bit guarded.

I couldn't blame him.

His job was literally to protect Ander, and in Ander's absence, he led the sector.

If Riley and I agreed to remain here, it would become my job to guard them all and essentially act as an enforcer.

Which I would do.

So long as they understood that Riley would always come first for me.

"First and foremost, I will expect appropriate protection for my mate. At *all* times." Which included her heat cycles.

Ander nodded. "We are in the process of developing suites to help mask scents. These suites are also being built with state-of-the-art technology that makes access by unauthorized users nearly impossible."

"That's why I mentioned having a secondary location,"

Elias said. "I would recommend either taking one of these suites full-time or maintaining it as a second home for special circumstances."

"Both of which we will offer," Ander added. "Dr. Campbell is bringing us a wealth of knowledge and expertise. We are willing to offer whatever you need to make your stay here permanent."

Elias dipped his chin, the two Alphas clearly in sync. I suspected they'd been friends for a while.

"I would like to review the suite option during our tour," I informed them both.

"Consider it ⸴ done," Ander replied, his eyebrow arching. "What else?"

I met his gaze and held it. "You will never reprimand my mate. If she does something that offends you, you inform me and I will handle her punishment."

Riley inhaled sharply beside me, causing me to look at her.

"We both know this is a requirement," I told her. "I won't let anyone discipline you except for me."

She bristled. "Who says I ever need to be disciplined?"

I merely stared at her until her cheeks turned a pretty pink.

"I'm not a pet meant to obey every order," she muttered.

"Never a pet," I agreed. "Just my feisty Omega who has no trouble bossing Alphas around."

"Only when they need a stern word," she returned.

I smiled and looked expectantly at Ander.

"Noted," he replied, still stoic.

Meanwhile, Elias seemed to be looking at Riley with a bit more adoration in his gaze.

Yeah, my Omega likes being a brat, I thought at him. *But she's* my *brat.*

"If anyone touches her in reprimand or otherwise, I will take that as a direct challenge. And that won't end well for anyone involved," I added, ensuring they heard and understood me.

I had no doubt Riley would one day piss off Ander.

She was all fiery energy and passion, while he exuded calm and maintained an unflappable air. That combination of personalities would either be a perfect match or end in conflict.

So I wanted it known now that he would not be the one to discipline her.

I would.

And only me.

"Noted," he repeated, this time with a bit more steel in his tone. "And if anyone touches Riley in this sector, they will have me to deal with as well."

"Likewise," Elias agreed.

I nodded. *That* was what I wanted to hear—an agreement to guard my mate as though she belonged to them, too. "Then my conditions have been met."

"That's it?" Riley asked incredulously. "A safe place for my heat cycle and the guarantee that only you can reprimand me?"

"Yes." I didn't elaborate beyond that single-worded reply, as there wasn't much else left to say.

"Seriously?" she pressed. "You're not even going to negotiate for a position?"

"My position is an enforcer," I told her. I didn't need Ander to tell me that. It was my natural role. "And I'll still be your guard. Always."

"But there's not much that can happen to me here," she argued. "They built a *dome*." She pointed upward like I didn't know what she meant.

It'd been a pretty impressive thing to fly through. The

glass-like structure had needed to be opened to allow our arrival. Apparently, it spanned the entire sector all the way to the ground.

There were some doors that allowed exterior access for when a shifter needed a good run, but it was extremely secure.

And it wasn't really glass but some high-tech substance with the texture of glass, which allowed for a pretty view of the surrounding mountains.

"The Infected are not the only threats out there," I reminded her. "But I agree—the security appeals to me."

She gave me a look. "The security means you're going to be bored."

"With you as my mate?" I smiled. "I'll never be bored. Besides, I imagine Ander will have tasks for me."

"I will," he said, not missing a beat. "Several."

Loyalty tests, I translated. His father might have put in a good word for me based on our previous interaction, but Ander would want me to prove my worth to him. "I look forward to it."

"Then I can't wait to introduce you to Enzo," he drawled, causing Elias to snort.

"One of your challengers?" I guessed.

Ander grunted. "If he can be called that."

Riley frowned. "Are you going to make Jonas fight?" Her scent changed, telling me that concerned her.

"I won't need to fight much, *ástin mín*," I promised. "Once or twice will establish the hierarchy."

She knew as well as I did that this part would be necessary. We were animals at heart. *Wolves.* Hierarchy was second nature to us all.

Her frown deepened.

"I doubt Ander has any vampires in his sector," I

added quietly. "And I grew up with V-Clan wolves. I'll be okay."

"I know. I just don't like thinking about you fighting after…" She trailed off.

I reached over to give her nape a little squeeze. "I beat that Viking Alpha. I doubt any of Ander's Alphas will rival him in size."

"Where the hell did you fight a Viking Alpha?" Elias asked, clearly intrigued.

"North Carolina." I didn't elaborate, as it wasn't a story I wished to discuss. "I can help with your challenger problem."

Ander's golden irises flickered with the first signs of emotion. Just a hint of cautious relief. "Then I'll introduce you to the pack."

"Already?" Riley asked with a gasp. "He'll fight today?"

I gave her nape another gentle squeeze. "I don't think he means today. We have to go on a tour first."

Ander didn't comment, something I appreciated. Other Alphas might have taken offense to Riley's tone. But he merely observed.

"Okay," she agreed, her blue eyes finding mine. "Tour first."

I leaned over and brushed a kiss against her cheek. "We'll find a proper nest."

She narrowed her gaze, making me grin.

"I'm your kept Alpha now," I added, smiling. "I want a nest to live in while you work."

Her nose crinkled.

Then she realized I was teasing her.

At least a little bit.

I did want a nest—just one with her. Maybe one day we would have pups. Maybe we wouldn't.

I would take the requisite pills to keep from procreating during her cycles. Unless she told me otherwise.

My life was with Riley.

Her happiness mattered most.

As evidenced by her smile now. It made my wolf come alive in response, my soul satisfied by my mate's pleasure.

"We'll build a nest," she told me, her eyes sparkling. "Together."

"Together," I agreed.

Her lips curled, and she looked at Ander again. "I think it's time for our tour of your sector, Alpha. My mate and I need to pick a new home."

I pulled her toward me and kissed her temple.

You make crash-landing a plane near an Infected nest worth all the pain and chaos in the world, I thought at her. *And I can't wait to see what fate has in store for us next.*

The End

Do you want more X-Clan? The full series is available now.

Curious about Kieran? He's the primary (anti)hero of *Blood Sector*, book one of the V-Clan series.

Blood Sector
A V-Clan Novel

Quinn McNamara

Blood. Death. War.
A dynasty destroyed.
Leaving me as the ultimate prize.

I'm an unmated Omega wolf. A Princess. And destined to rule. But the remaining Alpha Princes all want to claim me, their brutal methods terrifying and cruel.

I've spent the last century running, hiding in places where no one would think to look.
Only *he* found me. Prince Kieran, the most powerful shifter of them all.

Our game of hide-and-seek has come to an end.
It's time for me to submit.

Or to die fighting.

Kieran O'Callaghan

My little trickster escaped me once. She indulged in a dangerous game of chase throughout the sectors, but I've finally found my prize.

Poor little darling thought I valued chivalry and courting. I'm an Alpha Prince. I take what I want, when I want it, however I want it. And her sweet blood beckons the predator within me to destroy all her dreams of a happily-ever-after.

Let the Princes enjoy their Royal V-Wars.
As long as they bow to me as King of Blood Sector, I won't intervene.
Besides, I have a new pretty little Omega to tame. It's time to put a crown on her and make her my queen.

Author's Note: *This is a standalone dark shifter romance with Omegaverse themes. Kieran is an unapologetic Alpha Prince, and Quinn is a feisty Omega Princess. It's a match made in literal hell, where the antihero is the king.*

FIND ON AMAZON

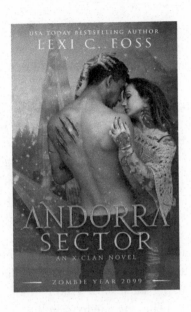

Andorra Sector
A standalone omegaverse Shifter Novel

Katriana Cardona

My life ended the moment the X-Clan found me.

Bitten.
Turned.
And claimed by *him*.

My genetic markers label me as a rare Omega. But inside,
I'm all female alpha. And I will not heel. Not even to the
Alpha of Andorra Sector.

Ander Cain promises me protection.
A new world of pleasure and pain.
But he wants all of me in return.
Even if it means taking me by force.

I'll be damned if I give up my inner fight. I spent the last twenty-one years battling the walking dead. These wolves won't know what hit them when I'm through.

Ander Cain

My life began the moment I found her, my darling little mate. She's the force of nature Andorra Sector needs to give us hope for a future. A reason to keep going and to protect our lands from the zombie infestation beyond.

Yet she refuses to play by our rules.

Born in a time where humans will do anything to survive, she's not used to the pack hierarchy or the laws our kind abides by. Oh, but she'll learn. And I'll thoroughly enjoy being the one to train her.

Katriana Cardona can fight me all she wants, but in the end, she will be mine. Whether she submits or not.

Note: This is a standalone shifter romance with omegaverse and dystopian elements. Certain content may be too dark for some readers, so please review the warning note inside if you have concerns.

LEXI C FOSS

USA Today Bestselling Author Lexi C. Foss loves to play in dark worlds, especially the ones that bite. She lives in Chapel Hill, North Carolina with her husband and their furry children. When not writing, she's busy crossing items off her travel bucket list, or chasing eclipses around the globe. She's quirky, consumes way too much coffee, and loves to swim.

Want access to the most up-to-date information for all of Lexi's books? Sign-up for her newsletter here.

Lexi also likes to hang out with readers on Facebook in her exclusive readers group - Join Here.

Where To Find Lexi:
www.LexiCFoss.com

ALSO BY LEXI C. FOSS

Blood Alliance Series - Dystopian Paranormal

Chastely Bitten

Royally Bitten

Regally Bitten

Rebel Bitten

Kingly Bitten

Cruelly Bitten

Blood Alliance Standalones - Dystopian Paranormal

Blood Day

Crave Me

Dark Provenance Series - Paranormal Romance

Heiress of Bael (FREE!)

Daughter of Death

Son of Chaos

Paramour of Sin

Princess of Bael

Captive of Hell

Elemental Fae Academy - Reverse Harem

Book One

Book Two

Book Three

Elemental Fae Queen

Winter Fae Queen

Hell Fae - Reverse Harem

Hell Fae Captive

Hell Fae Warden

Immortal Curse Series - Paranormal Romance

Book One: Blood Laws

Book Two: Forbidden Bonds

Book Three: Blood Heart

Book Four: Blood Bonds

Book Five: Angel Bonds

Book Six: Blood Seeker

Book Seven: Wicked Bonds

Book Eight: Blood King

Immortal Curse World - Short Stories & Bonus Fun

Elder Bonds

Blood Burden

Assassin Bonds

Mershano Empire Series - Contemporary Romance

Book One: The Prince's Game

Book Two: The Charmer's Gambit

Book Three: The Rebel's Redemption

Midnight Fae Academy - Reverse Harem

Ella's Masquerade

Book One

Book Two

Book Three

Book Four

Noir Reformatory - Ménage Paranormal Romance

The Beginning

First Offense

Second Offense

Third Offense

Underworld Royals Series - Dark Paranormal Romance

Happily Ever Crowned

Happily Ever Bitten

X-Clan Series - Dystopian Paranormal

Andorra Sector

X-Clan: The Experiment

Winter's Arrow

Bariloche Sector

V-Clan Series - Dystopian Paranormal

Blood Sector

Night Sector

Vampire Dynasty - Dark Paranormal

Violet Slays

Crossed Fates

Other Books

Scarlet Mark - Standalone Romantic Suspense

Rotanev - Standalone Poseidon Tale

Carnage Island - Standalone Reverse Harem Romance

Made in USA - Kendallville, IN
13811_9781685301446
05.04.2023 1339